Gone Wild

Garden Girls Series Book 2

Hope Callaghan

FIRST EDITION

Copyright © 2015

All rights reserved.

www.hopecallaghan.com

This book is a work of fiction. Although places mentioned may be real, the characters, names and incidents and all other details are products of the author's imagination and are used fictitiously. Any resemblance to actual events or actual persons, living or dead is purely coincidental.

No part of this publication may be copied, reproduced in any format, by any means, electronic or otherwise, without prior consent from the copyright owner and publisher of this book. The only exception is brief quotations in printed reviews.

TABLE OF CONTENTS

Chapter 1

Gloria Rutherford grabbed her broom off the side porch and began sweeping the small pile of brown leaves out of the corner. She stared up at the clear blue sky. Fall was a beautiful time of year to live in West Michigan. The changing seasons and cool fall days were something Gloria would never, ever tire of.

But today there was no time to reflect on how much she was enjoying the new season. She was trying to get ready for her much-anticipated company. Her grandsons Tyler and Ryan were coming for the weekend. The fact that they hadn't been over in quite some time and that her daughter Jill seemed overly-anxious about the visit made Gloria wonder if perhaps they would be a little too hard to handle...

She swept the last few leaves from the porch and shuffled over to prop the broom in the corner when something caught her eye. The tall weeds next to the edge of the barn were swaying back and forth, as if blowing in the wind or being moved by an unseen force. Which was more than a little odd considering there wasn't even the slightest of breezes.

She took a step down as her eyes wandered to the small set of doors on the far side of the barn. The door wasn't completely shut. It was open a good six inches.

Gloria was certain she hadn't left the door open. In fact, she couldn't remember the last time she'd actually used the side door. She grabbed her cell phone off the chair, shoved it into her back pocket and began walking in the direction of the barn. The boulder she used to keep the door closed had been rolled back. She side-stepped the boulder and pushed the door open, just far enough to stick her head inside. She stood there for a brief moment waiting for her eyes to adjust to the dim interior when she heard a faint creaking sound coming from inside, as if someone was stepping on a wooden floor. The only wooden floor in the barn was the loft.

She grabbed the shovel by the door, pushed the door open a little wider and squeezed through the narrow opening. Another hollow creak was followed by a distinct *ping,* as if a coin or small metal object had been dropped on the cement floor.

Gloria took a tentative step inside. "Hello?" She strained her ears. A second small creak echoed from the direction of the loft. She took another step forward. "Who's there?" She paused. A third creak closely followed the second. This one was even louder.

She stopped in her tracks. The thought of someone being inside the barn with her freaked her out. It was at that precise moment she began to have second thoughts about confronting a potential intruder.

Tires crunching on the gravel saved her from having to decide the best plan of action. She whirled around in time to catch a glimpse of her daughter's familiar blue Buick as it pulled into the drive.

Gloria cast a wary glance down the long center, past the milking parlor in the direction of

3

the loft before turning back. She quickly pulled the door shut and rolled the boulder back to its original spot.

By the time Gloria made it across the yard, the boys were already out of the car and barreling towards their beloved Grams. She wrapped them in a warm hug as she stared over the tops of their heads at her daughter, Jill.

After a quick hug, the boys took off in the direction of what used to be the pumpkin patch. Jill followed her mother inside the house, carrying the boys' backpacks as she went. She dropped them in the spare bedroom and made her way back out into the kitchen. "I hope they aren't too much of a handful," she fretted.

Gloria put her arm around her daughter's shoulders. "Now don't you worry about them one little bit. Go. Have a good time. We'll be just fine," she reassured her.

Moments later, Gloria watched as Jill's car pull out of the driveway. She turned around just in time to see Ryan bash one of the pumpkins on a nearby rock. He grabbed a handful of slimy

pumpkin guts in his fist and then smashed them in his older brother's face. Tyler didn't take too kindly to the gooey globs of seeds and slime clinging to his forehead and hair. He grabbed Ryan by the back of the neck and shoved his younger brother's face into what was left of the rotting pumpkin.

Gloria darted across the uneven garden as fast as her sneakers would allow, but it was too late. By the time she reached the battling boys, both were covered in the stringy, stinky substance. Tyler warily watched as his Grandmother approached. He leaned over to wrap a sticky arm around her when she took a small step back. "If you so much as lay a single finger on me with that goop," she warned, "I'll tie you to that big oak tree over there and leave you out here overnight."

Tyler's eyes widened in horror at the thought of being left outside all night by himself. He instantly dropped his arm to his side.

Gloria stuck a hand on her hip and pointed in the direction of the house. "Now get in that house and wash up," she commanded. "Both of you!"

The boys lowered their heads and shuffled towards the door. When Grams used that tone, they knew she meant business.

She slowly followed them inside. The uneasy feeling someone was in the barn returned as she cast a wary glance over her shoulder.

By the time the boys emerged from the shower with clean clothes and freshly scrubbed faces, Gloria had two glasses of cold milk and a plate of homemade chocolate brownies waiting.

The boys rushed to the kitchen table and were barely in their seats before they started scarfing down the entire plate. Ryan took a big gulp of milk as he studied his grandma. He could see she wasn't mad about the pumpkin smashing any longer so he thought he'd ask her what he'd been thinking about for days now. Ever since his mom told him they'd be staying at Gram's farm for the weekend. "Can we go play in the barn?"

Gloria's eyebrows furrowed. Only days earlier, she found odd items in the barn loft. As if someone had been hiding out in there. After seeing the side door open earlier today and hearing strange noises coming from the loft, she wasn't sure that was such a good idea.

But the boys were experts at wrapping their grandmother around their little finger. She just didn't have the heart to tell them no. Boys and barns just seemed to go together.

"Let me go check it out before I say yes." She threw on her sweater as she headed for the door. *Hopefully whoever was in there was long gone...*

She slowly made her way across the drive. She nervously wrapped her sweater around her thin frame. Never in her life had she ever been afraid of the barn but just the thought of a stranger taking up residence inside was downright frightening.

She unhooked the rusty metal latch and shifted her weight as she pushed on the heavy wooden door, forcing it down the weather-worn track that had been used for decades.

By the time the door was pushed all the way open, Gloria's heart was pounding loudly in her chest. She nervously rubbed her hands on the front of her jeans as she stepped inside.

Her silhouette cast a long shadow across the barn floor as the late afternoon sun poured in behind her. She stood for a moment. Not a sound could be heard except for the faint rustling of leaves that danced on the ground just outside the barn walls.

She took another step forward as her eyes scanned the interior of the barn. The faint smell of dark, rich earth and decades-old straw filled the air. The last time her husband, James, had been in the barn was almost two years ago – just days before he died unexpectedly.

The memory of that last time James ever stepped foot in the barn came rushing back. The strong smell of diesel filled the inside of the barn as Gloria waved a hand across her face. "How long are you going to keep that old bucket of bolts?"

James closed the cab door and slowly lowered himself to the barn floor. He patted a giant, mud-coated tire as he turned to his wife. "As long as old Bessie still runs and they haven't put me six feet under."

Gloria wrinkled her nose and shook her head at her husband. He didn't really farm the fields anymore. Hadn't in years, but she knew he loved to take the tractor out and wander over the acres of land as he reminisced about the old days. Every once in a blue moon Gloria would ride with him just so she could watch his eyes light up as he told her about the year the corn was knee high a month early. Or the time his beans grew ten times larger than that braggart Norman, whose farm was just down the road.

Yes, James loved the old farm even more than Gloria. He loved it with all his heart and lived there from the day he was born until the day he died.

Tears sprang up in her eyes as she reached out and put a worn hand on the side of the old Massey Ferguson.

"Grandma! Are you in here?"

Gloria quickly wiped away the lone tear that trickled down her cheek before turning to her grandson. "Over here Tyler."

Two sets of energetic feet pounded the barn floor as the boys raced over to where she was standing. A small hand reached up and grabbed hers. "So can we play in the barn?" She stared down at the bright green eyes that gazed up at her imploringly.

She nodded her head. There was no way she could tell them no. Not when Tyler looked at her like *that*.

"Before I let you play out here, I want to take a look around." Her gaze shifted to the loft. "Just to make sure there's nothing you shouldn't be getting into."

She took a step forward before turning around. "Stay right here until I'm done," she ordered firmly.

Gloria checked the loft first. At the top of the wooden ladder she stopped and studied the area carefully. Nothing appeared to be out of place. Nothing that is until she spied a clear spot on the middle of the floor where the straw had been swept aside.

She took a quick glance down to make sure the boys were still waiting where she left them before crawling over to the center of the loft. The old wooden boards were charred, as if someone had started a fire and then quickly put it out.

She made her way back down the narrow steps. She passed by the boys on the way to the milking parlor where she thoroughly checked every single stall. Next was a trip around the big metal tanks. She even lifted the wooden plank that ran down the center of the room.

Satisfied that everything was as it should be, she gave the boys the all clear to play inside. After instructing the boys not to jump from the loft, stab each other with pitchforks or try to crawl into the big metal milking tanks, she made her way back to the house.

Certain that there was no one inside the barn and that they couldn't get into *too* much trouble out there, Gloria began making supper. It was always so much more fun when she had someone to cook for.

Her phone rang just as she finished pushing a pan of homemade meatloaf and her famous baked macaroni and cheese into the oven. For a brief second she thought about not answering but what if it was Jill and she needed something?

"Hello?"

"Hi Gloria. How're you doing this afternoon?"

Gloria smiled as she recognized Andrea's voice on the other end. "Remember when we drove by that abandoned house in town on our way to lunch the other day?"

How could Gloria forget? "Yeah. The old Johnson mansion."

Andrea's voice bubbled with excitement. "Well, I started thinking about it. I did a little research and that house is for sale!"

That was news to Gloria. She'd never noticed a for sale sign in the yard...

"I did a little research on line," she went on. "I tracked down the owners and I'm thinking about putting an offer in on it."

Gloria had encouraged Andrea to move out of the city since she really seemed like a country girl at heart – but buying a major fixer upper? Not only that, but a fixer upper that was rumored to be haunted?

"Are you sure you're ready to take on a project like that, Andrea? I mean, that place needs a lot of work." She didn't want to burst her bubble but that place was in rough shape.

Andrea was bound and determined to at least take a look at it. "I was wondering if you had time, maybe we could go look at it together in the next day or two."

"How're we going to get in?" Gloria wondered aloud.

"Believe it or not, the owner sent me the keys – told me to go ahead and let myself in."

Gloria was shocked. "You're kidding."

"They seem like nice people and pretty desperate to get rid of the place. So can you?"

Gloria pulled the curtain aside as she glanced out the window. "My grandsons are staying with me for a couple days."

"Oh, they can come, too..." she interrupted.

"I don't know about that. These two can be a handful..." Gloria argued.

But Andrea would not take no for an answer. She was too excited. "Maybe we can go tomorrow after church?"

Gloria quickly caved. There was no reason to tell her no. Not only that, she was curious to see the inside of the house herself. After all, it wasn't very often you had a chance to check out a haunted house. "Yes. Yes, we can do that. But don't get your hopes up too high, Andrea. You haven't seen this place yet."

Gloria's warning went in one ear and out the other. "Great. It's settled then. We'll go check it out tomorrow."

At that precise moment, Gloria caught a glimpse of Tyler through the window. He was rounding the corner of the barn. There was a long, squirming snake dangling from his hand. Just ahead of him was his younger brother, Ryan, running for his life and screaming bloody murder.

"Look, I gotta go. My grandson's running through the yard holding onto what appears to be a rather large snake." And with that, Gloria was gone.

Andrea shook her head as she stared at the phone in her hand. *Poor Gloria. Sounds like she has her hands full!*

Gloria shoved her feet into a pair of nearby flip-flops, flung open the door and raced down the steps. Her first thought was *I need to put a pair of running shoes on with these two around.* Her second thought was, *I hope that snake is long gone by the time I reach the boys.* By the time she rounded the back side of the barn, it was close to what she'd hoped for. Tyler was no longer taunting his brother with the slithering reptile. The boys had somehow managed to find a large plastic bucket. The snake was inside with the lid safely on top.

They calmly looked up as Gloria approached. "Hey Grams." Ryan pointed a small, grubby finger at the bucket. "We found a pet. Can we keep him?"

Gloria shuddered as she stared down at the bucket. The outline of a rather large snake was clearly visible. There was no way she was going to let the boys keep the snake and she was certain that Jill would never allow it.

It was time to figure out if the snake was poisonous. "What does the snake look like?"

He's blue and he's this long." Ryan stretched his arms to about 3 feet.

Tyler shook his head. "No he's not, Ryan. He's shiny and gray!"

None of that sounded good, especially if Tyler was right.

"And he was slippery." Tyler held out a filthy palm. "He almost slipped right out of my hand." Forget the fact that he was racing across the field at the time...

Now Gloria was really frightened. She crouched down and placed both hands on the lid, making sure it was securely in place. She grabbed the handle and made her way over to the edge of the garden.

The boys followed right behind her, keeping a close eye on the bucket and their grandma, not completely convinced she wasn't just going to let their new pet escape.

She cautiously placed the bucket on the ground and turned to her young grandsons. "Here's what we're going to do. First we're going to get cleaned up – again! After that we're going to eat dinner," she went on. "And when we're done eating, you two are going to get on Gram's computer and find a picture of the snake. We need to know exactly what kind he is before we decide what to do with him. Agreed?"

Two small blonde heads bobbed up and down in unison. She shooed them inside. "Now get going!" The boys raced into the house taking the steps two at a time.

Gloria shuddered at the ominous white bucket perched in her yard before slowly following them indoors.

The boys couldn't wait for dinner to end as they argued about what they were going to name their new "pet."

Ryan shoved a fork full of baked macaroni and cheese in his mouth. "I think we should call him Slinky."

Tyler swung his feet back and forth under the table as he contemplated the snake's name. "What about Barney since we found him in the barn?"

Gloria didn't have the heart to tell them that there was no way on earth their mother was ever going to let them keep a snake but she had a feeling she wouldn't have to worry about that soon enough. If Tyler was right in describing the snake, they had a Blue Racer on their hands. They weren't venomous but they did have a nasty bite. Gloria had no idea what she would do then but no sense in worrying about it until she had to.

The boys inhaled the rest of their dinner and raced from the table to the computer. They quickly flipped it on and started researching the snakes. Gloria could hear them arguing as they looked at all the different pictures. Finally, they seemed to agree on one. "Hey Grams. We found our snake," Ryan called out.

Gloria finished putting the dishes away. She dried her hands and hung her apron on the hook by the door before walking over to the computer desk. Ryan pointed at the picture on the screen. "This is Slinky."

Gloria popped on her reading glasses and studied the picture. Just as she suspected. They both agreed it was a Blue Racer. "So neither of you got bit?"

The boys both shook their head no. "Nope."

"Well, that's a good thing since it would probably be hurting right about now." Jill would totally freak when she found out about the snake.

"Does that mean we can't keep him?" Tyler was deeply disappointed.

Gloria shook her head. "I'm afraid not. Blue Racers aren't meant to be house pets. They're supposed to live free out in the fields."

Ryan frowned and stuck his chin on his fist. "So we have to let him go?"

Gloria nodded her head. "Yes. Tomorrow."

She leaned down to look her grandsons in the eye. "Under no circumstances are you to go near the snake until then. OK?"

Both nodded in unison. "We won't Grams. We promise."

Bedtime finally rolled around, much to Gloria's relief and the boys' dismay. She tucked them in and listened as they said their prayers.

"Please God, can we keep our snake and take him home?" Tyler whispered. "We promise to take good care of him and make sure he doesn't get loose and scare Mom."

Gloria smiled as she heard his fervent little prayer. It was a good thing God didn't give us our hearts content, especially when it came to little boys.

She turned off the light and pulled the door slowly shut. "See you in the morning."

"Night grams. Love you," Tyler called out. "Thanks for having us over. We had a great time!" he added.

Gloria checked all the doors before heading to bed herself. She flipped on the small light over the stove before leaving the kitchen – just in case the boys woke up during the night and needed a drink of water.

Gloria pulled o her pajamas and crawled under the covers. She was just settling in when she felt something soft and furry rubbing against her feet. She lifted her head and looked down at the end of the bed. The covers were moving. Seconds later, Puddles' head emerged. "So this is where you've been hiding out!" It was the first time Gloria had seen her cat all day. The minute Puddles discovered the boys were in the house, he

21

hightailed it out of the kitchen and made himself scarce.

She scratched his ears and chin as he started to purr. "I know you don't like those two boys but they didn't mean to scare you, Puddles." He rubbed his head against her hand and then licked her palm. "Even so, it's probably safer for you to keep a low profile while they're here. Just in case."

Gloria laid her head on her pillow before saying her own prayers. "Thank you God for the good day you've given us. Thank you for a chance to spend some time with my grandsons and thank you that they didn't pick up a poisonous snake today." Kids could sure make you thankful in a real hurry. "Please give us a safe day tomorrow, one where the boys don't get hurt and I don't have to take make a trip to the emergency room. Amen."

Puddles curled into a tight ball and settled in right next to Gloria's head. The sound of his purring put her right to sleep – or maybe it was all the action that her grandsons had created that day. Either way, seconds later she was out like a light.

"Grams!! Come quick!!!"

Gloria bolted upright in bed. The room was pitch black except for a thin sliver of light beaming through the crack in the open door. She could barely make out the shadowy figure of her youngest grandson, Ryan. She glanced over at the clock beside her bed. It was 3:00 a.m.

She shook her head as if to clear it. Her foggy brain was still half asleep. "What are you doing out of bed?"

Instead of answering, he darted past the doorway, back towards the living room. "You gotta come! Quick!"

Gloria slid out of bed, slipped into a pair of slippers and threw on her robe as she grabbed her glasses off the nightstand. She rushed in the direction of her grandson's voices coming from the kitchen.

"What's going on? What's wrong?" Her eyes darted around the room frantically.

She spied Tyler kneeling on a chair underneath the kitchen window. He put a small finger to his lips. "Shhh!!" He pointed toward the barn. "Look! Someone's out there!"

Gloria leaned forward as she glanced over the boys head in the direction of the barn. Sure enough, there was a solitary light bobbing its way toward the big barn doors. She could barely make out a silhouette. The dark, shadowy figure was walking at a quick pace.

When the light reached the barn door, it paused for a moment. The barn door opened a crack, just far enough to let someone slip inside. Seconds later, the door closed and the light was gone.

Gloria swallowed hard. Someone was definitely in the barn. She picked up the phone and dialed 911. "Yes. This is Gloria Rutherford. I live at 276 Millington Drive in Belhaven. I just watched someone sneak into the barn on my property."

The 911 operator repeated the address and then told her an officer had been dispatched, assuring her he should be there within 10 minutes.

"You two stay here while I get dressed," Gloria whispered in a loud voice. "And I mean stay here – don't you dare even open this door," she warned.

She darted back to the bedroom and hastily threw on the nearest thing she could find. An old pair of sweatpants and a t-shirt she kept around for gardening. She glanced down at her mismatched outfit. *Well, it's not like I'm trying to impress a police officer.*

She quickly headed back to the kitchen. The boys were still peering out the window. "See anyone come out of the barn?"

The boys shook their heads in unison. "Nope."

Just then, a patrol car turned into the driveway and pulled up next to the garage. Gloria flipped on the porch light as she made her way outside, her grandsons right on her heels.

The officer stepped from his car and began walking toward the light. Gloria's eyes grew wide as the figure got closer. It was Officer Kennedy!

He recognized her at exactly the same moment. "Well if it isn't Gloria Rutherford."

Gloria ran a quick hand through her hair, certain at least half of it was standing straight up in the air. "Hello, Officer Kennedy."

He smiled as he made his way over to the familiar figure. She looked a lot younger with messy hair and sweatpants on.

He glanced around as he remembered the reason for his visit. "Dispatch said you saw someone creep into your barn?"

Ryan peeked out from behind his grandma as he grabbed her hand in a tight grip. "Me 'n Tyler saw him first." He pointed back at the kitchen window. "We saw him in the driveway and then we woke Grams up."

Kennedy smiled down at the earnest little face. "Let me go check it out."

Ryan took a step forward, as if to follow Officer Kennedy. "But you have to stay here," he told him. He looked up at Gloria. "To protect your Grandma."

Ryan stopped in his tracks. He nodded solemnly at the man in uniform.

Kennedy grabbed a heavy duty flashlight from the trunk of his patrol car and made his way over to the big red barn.

Gloria held her breath as he slowly opened the double doors and shined a beam of light inside. Seconds later, Kennedy disappeared into the darkness. The three of them caught a glimpse of his bright light bouncing around through the cracks in the barn walls.

After what seemed like an eternity, he finally stepped out of the barn and carefully closed the door. He disappeared from sight as he made his way around the backside. It seemed like he was gone forever before eventually making his way back over to where Gloria and the boys were standing.

"There isn't anyone inside. It's possible they got spooked when I pulled up."

He went on. "There's a pretty big gap on the back side of the barn where someone could easily squeeze through and escape out the other side."

He shook his head. "You really should padlock those doors and nail that back panel shut."

Gloria had been meaning to do just that but with everything that was going on, it completely slipped her mind. "I'll take care of it tomorrow," she promised.

Tyler piped up. "I'll make sure Grams does it," he assured the officer.

Officer Kennedy nodded solemnly at Tyler. "I'll hold you to that."

Gloria tugged on the bottom of her old t-shirt self-consciously. "Would you like to come in for a cup of coffee?"

Officer Kennedy smiled, the corners of his eyes crinkling up in a nice way. He shook his head. "Unfortunately, I'm on duty and have another call to follow up on."

He opened the patrol car door. "But maybe I could take you up on that offer some other day," he added.

Good thing it was nice and dark outside. Gloria blushed right down to her scalp.

Ryan tugged on Gloria's arm. "We can't tomorrow. We're going to visit a haunted house."

Kennedy's eyebrows shot up as he looked over at Gloria. "You're not working on another case, are you?"

Gloria blushed a deep red for the second time in a row. "No. Just going to take a look at a house my friend is thinking about buying." She turned to Ryan. "We don't know that it's haunted."

"But we think it is, right Grams?" Ryan insisted.

She ruffled his hair as she grinned at Kennedy. "We shall see."

Kennedy slid into the driver's seat. "You all have a good night and don't hesitate to call if you see anything else out there." He pointed in the direction of the barn.

Gloria watched the police car's tail lights disappear in the dark before making her way back inside. She was surprised at how deeply disappointed she was that he couldn't come in.

She nudged the boys. "Off to bed you two!"

It was several long hours before Gloria settled back down after the middle-of-the-night fright. Her mind went back and forth between being worried someone had taken up residence in her barn and wondering if she'd see Officer Kennedy again and if he would actually take her up on that cup of coffee.

Chapter 2

The next day dawned bright and early, mainly because the boys were up at sun rise, looking forward to another day of adventure and excitement, especially considering they would be visiting a haunted house.

Gloria waited until the boys were settled at the breakfast table before she picked up the phone to call Andrea. "Did you still want to check out the old Johnson house today?"

Andrea was nearly beside herself with excitement. She barely slept a wink the night before. That house was all she could think about. "Yes, of course! Do you still have your grandsons?"

"Yep. They'll have to come with us."

"Oh, that's fine with me." Andrea didn't care who came with them as long as she got to see the inside of that house.

Gloria looked over at the boys. She wasn't so sure Andrea would be saying that after she spent the afternoon with them... "We're getting ready for church now. We can have lunch here and then head over there afterwards."

"That's perfect. I can hardly wait," Andrea gushed.

Gloria didn't have the heart to burst her bubble. Once she saw the condition of the house, she was probably going to change her mind.

The boys were done eating by now. She shooed them off to get ready as she loaded the dishwasher and made her way to her room.

By the time Gloria and the boys got to church, Andrea was already waiting outside. Justin, one of the handsome young ushers, had her ear bent. Gloria shook her head. She'd never seen him so *interested* in a female. He sure seemed taken by Andrea.

Andrea finally caught Gloria's eye. She waved her over. Justin's face fell when he saw Gloria and the boys walk towards them. "Good morning, Justin."

"Good morning, Mrs. Rutherford," he politely replied. "Will the boys be going to Sunday School?"

She patted Ryan's head as she nodded firmly. "Yes, they will."

Justin reluctantly said good-bye to Andrea as he led the boys in the direction of the youth building. He glanced back longingly as Gloria and Andrea headed inside. "Justin sure does seem to be taken with you."

Andrea shook her head. "He was talking my ear off." She shrugged. "I don't believe I've ever met a man who likes to talk as much as he does!"

Gloria scanned the pews before finally spying Ruth in the back. Ruth slid down the bench as she made room for two more. Her other friends, Margaret and Lucy, were on the other side.

This week's message was about supporting the missionaries the church sponsored. Several of the husband/wife teams made their way to the pulpit and shared their stories of souls saved in third world countries like Honduras. Gloria dabbed

33

at her eyes when they told the congregation about all the poor, hungry children living in dirt huts, walking miles by foot just to hear about Jesus and then giving their lives to Christ.

The small group of Garden Girls assembled outside after the service. "I have to skip the neighborhood deliveries today," Gloria explained. She glanced over at Andrea. "Andrea wants to run over and take a look at the old Johnson mansion. She's thinking about buying it."

Gasps of shock went round the small circle. "That place should be condemned!" Ruth declared.

But Andrea wouldn't hear of it. "Oh, I only got a quick glimpse of the outside but I know it can be restored to its original beauty. I'm thinking about fixing it up and moving in," she added, excitement filling her voice.

Dot patted Andrea's hand. "Dear, I can see the stars in your eyes as you talk about that old place. Just remember to keep your eyes wide open as you look around."

She turned to Gloria. "You'll make sure she's not getting in over her head?"

Gloria nodded. "Of course. That's one of the reasons I'm going with her." She put an arm around Andrea's shoulder. "To keep her feet on the ground and be the voice of reason."

Tyler and Ryan rushed over to where they were standing. "Are we going to go look at the haunted house now?"

Gloria shook her head. "First we have a quick lunch and then we go look at it."

Andrea followed Gloria back to the farm. As soon as they were out of the car, Tyler took off for the other side of the garden in the direction of the plastic pail so he could check on his "pet." Ryan was right on his heels. The boys came to an abrupt halt as they stared down at the empty pail in disbelief. Tyler tipped the pail sideways and peered inside. "Barneys gone!"

Gloria tiptoed past the edge of the garden as she made her way over to where the boys were standing. Sure enough, the plastic pail was empty.

Tyler held the lid in his hand as tears welled up in his eyes. "The lid was just sitting on top!"

Hmmm, Gloria thought. So someone took the lid off and let the snake go.... Maybe the same person who was in the barn last night.

She wasn't the only one thinking that. "Grams, whoever was in the barn last night must've let Barney go."

Andrea was standing beside them now and caught the tail end of what Ryan just said. "Someone was in the barn last night?"

Andrea was the one that discovered someone had been in Gloria's barn in the first place when she stumbled upon a blanket and navy blue backpack in the loft. Lucy's boyfriend, Bill, searched the barn the next day but the loft was empty. The only thing that turned up was a small pocket knife tucked away under a pile of straw. A knife that Gloria didn't recognize.

She promised Andrea she would put padlocks on the doors but had forgotten all about it.

When she finally did remember, she kept finding excuses to put it off.

Andrea marched over to the barn door. She stuck a hand on her hip as she turned back to stare accusingly at a sheepish Gloria. "You promised me you were going to get locks on these."

"I know, I know. I just got busy. I have a couple locks in the garage I can use."

"Good!" Andrea replied firmly. "We'll do that after we change our clothes and eat lunch. Before we go look at my house," she added.

Gloria sighed when she heard Andrea say, "My house." She never realized her young friend had such a stubborn streak. Maybe that was a good thing, considering all she'd been through...

Back inside, Gloria threw together a quick lunch of grilled cheese sandwiches and tomato soup. She warmed the leftover macaroni and cheese from the night before and set it on the table along with the soup and sandwiches.

Andrea rubbed her hands together. "Oohh. This macaroni and cheese looks delicious!"

Tyler eyed Andrea suspiciously as he scooped a large spoonful onto his plate, making sure he got his fair share. "Grams makes the best macaroni and cheese in the whole world!"

Gloria caught a glimpse of Puddles' head as he peeked out from around the corner of the dining room door. The tantalizing smell of food filled the air as he sniffed appreciatively. He stopped short of actually slinking into the kitchen when he spotted Tyler and Ryan sitting at the table.

Gloria broke off a piece of her sandwich and made her way into the dining room. She rounded the corner to find Puddles hovering under the hutch. She broke off a piece of the cheesy bread and held it out to her furry friend. Puddles sniffed the offering for just a second before wolfing it down in one bite. The second piece she held out was gone just as fast.

Gloria patted his head and gave him a quick stroke on the back before heading back into the kitchen.

"Was that Puddles?" Andrea would've loved to see the cat before she left.

38

"Yeah," Gloria answered. "Unfortunately, he won't come out while the boys are here." She went on. "Last time they visited, the boys tried flushing poor Puddles down the toilet and now he's terrified to come out when they're around."

"Gram's, we promised we wouldn't do that again."

"I know, Ryan, but Puddles doesn't understand."

After lunch, they all changed out of their Sunday attire and into clothes that were a little more appropriate for rummaging around abandoned houses.

By the time Gloria made her way back into the kitchen, Andrea and the boys were already waiting by door.

"So where are those locks?" Andrea was not going to let it go.

On the way to the barn, they stopped by the garage and grabbed two heavy duty padlocks, a hammer and some barn nails.

They slowly pushed the large double doors open and stepped inside. Tyler was the first to make it through the door. He turned to Ryan. "C'mon, let's go." Gloria stuck her arm out so fast she nearly clothes-lined them. "Not so fast! We need to make sure there's no one in here before you run off."

Andrea walked over to the wooden ladder and slowly climbed to the top. "No one up here."

Gloria made her way over to the milking parlor and stepped down. She let her eyes adjust for a moment as she carefully studied the room. "All clear."

The boys scrambled to the top of a stack of hay bales. "No one back here, either," Tyler announced.

With the all-clear, the boys headed for the loft as Gloria and Andrea made their way around the outside of the barn, checking each section carefully for loose boards where someone would be able to slip through and crawl inside. For the most part, the barn was secure but there was one section on the back side where a large board was hanging on by one lone nail. On closer inspection, it looked like someone had intentionally popped the nails out.

Gloria pulled a long metal nail out of her pocket and placed it firmly against the faded red plank.

"Can I do that?" Gloria looked over to see Andrea gazing at her anxiously.

"You want to?"

Andrea stepped forward and reached for the hammer. "Yes!"

Gloria handed her a couple nails before taking a step back. Andrea made quick work of securing the board. In fact, she put more nails in the board than was probably necessary but Gloria didn't have the heart to stop her. She was obviously enjoying herself.

After checking the rest of the barn's exterior, the two made their way back inside to check on the boys. It was awfully quiet inside. When Gloria got to the door, she could see the boys were still in the loft. Well, one of the boys was up in the loft. Her oldest grandson, Tyler, was *swinging* from a beam as Ryan stood at the ledge and egged him on. "Jump! Jump!"

Gloria eyes dropped to the barn floor. There was a loose pile of hay directly below where Tyler was hanging. It would more than likely soften the fall but not necessarily stop her young grandson from breaking something.

"Don't you dare, Tyler Adams!" Gloria took a step forward. "Get down from there this instant!" she demanded.

Tyler recognized that tone and immediately started to pull himself back towards the loft when he began to lose his grip. His fingers slipped from their hold as he dangled by one lone arm. Andrea and Gloria watched in helpless horror. The seconds ticked by until finally, when he couldn't hold on a second longer, he fell straight down and hit the hay with a loud *thud*.

Gloria rushed over to where her grandson lay sprawled out on the barn floor, a dazed look on his face. She leaned over his small frame. "Tyler are you OK?"

42

For a moment he stared up at Gloria, a blank expression covered his face.

Ryan scampered down the ladder and stood over his older brother. "Dude, that was cool!"

Tyler glanced over at his brother, his eyebrows drawn together, a confused expression on his face. "Who are you?"

Gloria started to feel light-headed. Tyler must've hit his head and now he didn't recognize them! "Quick, we need to get him in the car and take him to the emergency room!"

Andrea made a dash for the door.

Just then, Tyler jumped to his feet and burst out laughing. "Ha-ha! Psyche!"

He brushed off his jeans. "Grams, I'm fine." He looked up at the beam he'd just been dangling from. "Man, that was fun! I wish I could do it again!"

Gloria wanted to strangle her grandson at that very moment and give him a real reason to have to go to the hospital.

Andrea marched over to Tyler and grabbed his arm. "You nearly gave your grandmother a heart attack! Apologize right this instant!"

Tyler actually looked contrite as he reached for his grandmother's shaky hand. "I'm sorry Gram's. I didn't mean to scare you."

Gloria took a deep breath and pulled her grandson close. "I thought you were really hurt."

Ryan made his way over to her other side as he wrapped two small arms around her waist. "We're sorry Grams. We won't do it again. We'll be good!"

Gloria held them tight as she sent up a silent prayer of gratitude to God neither were hurt. "Unfortunately for you two, that stunt means the barn is off limits for the rest of the time that you're here," she said firmly.

The boys let go and looked up at their grandmother glumly. She was using that tone. There was no sense in trying to convince her to change her mind.

The four of them made their way outside. Gloria pushed the doors shut and snapped the lock in place with a firm click.

Andrea could no longer contain her excitement. "Ready to go?" She dangled a set of ancient-looking keys from her fingertips.

Ryan reached up and touched one of the long, skinny keys. "Wow, those things look weird."

Gloria walked over and examined the ring. "Why those are old skeleton keys."

Andrea jingled them around on her finger. "I can hardly wait to find out if they work!"

The four of them hopped into Anabelle and rolled out onto the main road. Moments later they pulled up in front of the Johnson place. The place was in even rougher shape than Gloria remembered. Long vines wound around the rusty metal fence. The gates looked as if they hadn't been opened in decades.

Andrea swallowed hard. Keys in hand, she grabbed the door handle. "Guess I better unlock the gate."

"I'll go with you!" Before she could reply, Ryan scrambled out of the backseat and onto the side of the road. He bravely reached for Andrea's hand as they made their way over to the gate.

She tried four different keys and none of them fit. She was darned near ready to give up when the fifth key finally fit. The rusty metal frame groaned loudly in protest as it reluctantly opened. Chunks of thick rust fell to the ground as the gate rubbed hard against the corroded hinges.

Andrea and Ryan dragged the door open, just far enough for Gloria to squeeze Anabelle through the gate and onto the bumpy gravel drive. Gloria turned the wheel and rounded the corner. Tall, majestic oaks lined the narrow path leading up to the front of the house.

Gloria grabbed a couple flashlights from the glove box and gingerly stepped down onto what was at one time a lush, manicured lawn. She shuffled through the thick weeds, praying there were no snakes in the near vicinity and came up behind where the other three were now standing.

The four of them had a clear view of what was once a majestic, stately home. Faded wooden shutters covered every single window facing the front of the house. There were several gaping holes in the sprawling upper deck where the floorboards were either rotted out or missing. Gloria looked straight up through the gaping holes at the clear blue sky above.

Andrea swallowed hard and took a step forward. "Guess we better go check it out, huh." Gloria and the boys followed close behind.

The first key she inserted fit perfectly and surprisingly enough, the lock turned with ease. The door swung open effortlessly without a single, solitary protest.

The foursome stepped inside and gazed around in awe. A solid marble staircase flowed from both sides of the upper level, joined in the center and then continued down to the grand entry. The intricate wrought iron spindles were capped with a solid mahogany handrail.

To the right of the entry was a large, open room with soaring ceilings and an ornate dining

47

table. An antique brass chandelier hung above the large piece of furniture.   To the left was what appeared to be a formal living room, complete with a massive, hand-carved fireplace that filled up at least half the outer wall. Slipcovers masked multiple pieces of furniture. Solid wooden legs peeked out from beneath the heavy covers.

"This place is perfect!" Andrea exclaimed.

Gloria had to admit it was pretty cool. The inside appeared to be in a lot better condition than she ever could have imagined.

The small group veered to the right as they wandered through the dining room, making their way to the back of the house. A generous-sized Butler's Pantry connected the dining room to the kitchen.

Andrea pushed the heavy swinging door aside as she made her way into the kitchen. Gloria shook her head as she looked around. This house was loaded with surprises. The kitchen was filled with bright sunlight beaming in through large, leaded glass windows that covered two walls on the back side of the kitchen. The kitchen was definitely dated. Everything in it appeared to be original from when it was built but it was clean. Almost too clean.

"Didn't you say the owners hadn't been in this place for years?" Gloria walked over and swiped a hand across the tile countertop. "Not a spot of dust. It looks like someone just cleaned this."

She reached over and turned on the kitchen faucet. Clean, clear water poured out. "If this hasn't been used in years, wouldn't the water be rusty?"

The Sherlock Holmes in her perked up. There was more to this place than met the eye. She glanced around the cupboards and poked her head inside the fridge. It was empty but something still wasn't adding up.

Andrea looked around uncertainly. "You don't think someone is living in here..."

Gloria patted her arm. "I'm not trying to frighten you. Just curious about some things..."

They circled around through the cozy library on the other side of the kitchen as they made their way into the large living room before eventually ending up back in the entry.

The massive staircase was wide enough for all four of them to climb the steps side-by-side. When they reached the center landing, they paused for just a moment before deciding to head to the right.

Tyler tugged on Gloria's hand. He pointed to the opposite wing of the house. "Gram, can we go explore over there?"

She shook her head absentmindedly. "I'd rather you not do that. Not until I've had a chance to look around first."

A quick tour of the right wing revealed several small bedrooms and baths, all filled with antique furnishings and original fixtures. They crossed over to the left hand side where there were two small bedrooms and an adjoining bath. Directly behind the two solid oak six panel doors at the end of the hall was a luxurious master suite. Andrea gasped when she saw how large and grandiose the room was. There was an intimate sitting area tucked into the corner. Windows on all three sides of the quaint sitting room looked out onto a private courtyard below. There wasn't a walk-in master closet but rather a wall of closets that ran the length of an entire section. It even had a massive stone fireplace.

"Where's the bathroom?" Ryan was hopping around on one foot. "I gotta go."

They looked around the room. There was no master bath.

"Go use the hall bath but come right back," Gloria warned.

Andrea was deeply disappointed. "Why wouldn't they put a master bath in here?"

It did seem more than a little odd not to have one. That meant the owners would have to use a hall bath. Unless...

Gloria wandered over to the far side of the fireplace. She looked up at the ceiling. Intricate cream-colored crown moulding covered the perimeter. There was one spot where the detailing had a clean, straight line cut through. She followed the cut mark down the side of the wall.

She moved over to stand just below the mark. Maybe, just maybe… She pressed lightly on the wall. Suddenly, the wall swung open.

Ryan was already back from the bathroom break. "Grams found a secret door!" He rushed over to stand beside Gloria.

On the other side of the bedroom wall was a spectacular master bath. The walls were covered in crimson velvet wallpaper. A gleaming brass chandelier hung directly over an enormous jetted tub. Decorative ceramic tiles lined the walls surrounding the tub. An oversized walk-in shower was just to the left. The water closet was tucked away on the right. On both sides of the large room were solid marble vanities with shiny brass fixtures.

Andrea peeked over Gloria's shoulder. "Oh my gosh! I'm sold!"

She walked slowly around the bath, running her hand across the counters in awe. "This place is amazing. Gloria, I'm going to buy it!"

Her eyes were shining as she looked back at her friend. "I'm going to restore this mansion to its glory days!"

It seemed like a lot of work to Gloria but Andrea was young and she apparently had the money to take on a project of this magnitude.

Still... "Maybe you should have a contractor come by here and give you some quotes. You know, just so you'll have some kind of idea how much work and money a place like this is going to cost to fix up..."

Gloria could see her words were falling on deaf ears. Andrea was in love with this house!

Just then her cell phone beeped. Jill sent a text message asking her mom to call her right away. The signal on Gloria's cell phone was almost non-existent inside the massive mansion. "I'm going to step outside and call Jill."

"Great," Andrea chimed in, "I'm going to take a walk around the property before we leave."

The boys followed Grams outside as Andrea headed around the corner of the house, past the overgrown hedge that surrounded the home's exterior.

Gloria dialed Jill's number. The boys decided that swinging on the open metal entrance gate looked like fun. She shook her head "no" but the boys ignored her.

"Hey Jill."

"Hey Mom, how's it going with the boys?"

Gloria motioned at them to get down but it was too late. Ryan was hung up, literally, on the outside of the gate, his feet dangling in the air.

Gloria walked over and using her one free arm, gave her grandson a lift, helping free him from the metal pin. "Oh, we're doing fine. Just hanging around."

Tyler dissolved in a fit of laughter when he caught what Grams just said.

Jill sounded relieved. "We're running a little late. We probably won't be able to pick the boys up until after dinner," she continued. "I hope that's ok..."

"Oh, no problem. We're looking at the old Johnson mansion..."

"Really – isn't that place haunted or something?"

Just then, Andrea tore around the corner of the house, her eyes wide with fear. She motioned frantically. "Gloria, come quick!"

"Listen Jill, I have to go. I'll see you later." Gloria hung up the phone and made a fast path in the direction of Andrea. The boys were hot on her heels.

When she rounded the corner, she spied Andrea standing in front of a small garden shed. The door was wide open and she was pointing inside.

Gloria cautiously made her way over to the door and peered in. There was a large green tarp draped in the far corner. Dangling from the outer edge of the tarp was a hand. A human hand.

Tyler squeezed around his grandmother to get a look inside. "What's that?"

Gloria clamped a hand over his eyes as she pulled him away from the doorway. "Ryan, don't look in there!" she ordered.

Andrea slammed the door shut. She stared at Gloria, an expression of pure horror frozen on her face. "We need to call the police."

Gloria nodded, her hand still tightly pressed against her grandson's eyes.

It wasn't long before the squeal of sirens could be heard. Seconds later, several emergency vehicles came to a screeching halt just outside the gate.

Officer Joe Nelson was the first to make his way over to the shed.

Andrea pointed inside. "In there."

Joe slowly pushed the wooden door open and peeked around the corner. He turned back around. "Maybe it would be best if you wait out front."

Gloria nodded. There was no way she wanted the boys to see this.

As they made their way back to the front, the rest of the cavalry rushed to the back yard.

"Was that a real body Grams?"

Gloria slowly nodded. "It would appear so, Tyler."

Officer Joe found them several minutes later, perched on the staircase just inside the door. He looked at the boys but spoke to Andrea and Gloria. "I need to ask you a few questions..."

"Boys, go outside and play for a minute – but don't go anywhere near the shed. Stay out front," Gloria instructed firmly.

Joe watched as the boys scampered out the door. He pulled a small spiral notepad and pen from this pocket. "Who found the body?"

Andrea raised her hand. "It was me."

"Just curious, how did you two get in here?" He looked around. "This place has been empty for as long as I can remember."

"I-I'm thinking about buying it," Andrea replied weakly. "The owner mailed me the keys so I could take a look inside."

"They live out of state," she added.

Joe tapped his ballpoint pen on the open notepad in his hand. "From what we can tell, the body hasn't been here long. Probably less than 24 hours."

Gloria swallowed hard. *What if they'd shown up earlier and come face-to-face with the killer leaving the body in the shed?*

The girls caught a glimpse of the paramedics as they walked past the front door, carrying a stretcher. A shroud of white was draped loosely over the body.

One of the fireman took a step inside. "There were a couple personal items on the floor next to the body. Stuff that looks like it doesn't belong in an old gardening shed."

Joe flipped the pad shut and shoved it back in his pocket. "What kind of stuff?"

"A flashlight, a dark blue backpack."

Andrea and Gloria stared at each other. *A dark blue backpack.*

Andrea needed to get a good look at that backpack. "Now that the body's gone, can we take a look in the shed?"

"As long as you don't touch anything," Joe warned.

Before he could change his mind, Andrea quickly jumped to her feet. "We won't. We promise."

They retraced their steps back to the shed. Gloria gently pushed the door open. The girls peered inside. Sure enough, there was a navy blue backpack in the corner.

Was this the same backpack that Andrea saw in Gloria's barn a couple weeks ago? She didn't dare ask the question in front of Joe but the look Andrea gave her was answer enough. It was more than likely the same one.

"Unless you need us for something else, we're going to lock up the house and head out." Gloria nodded over at the boys who were darting around the firemen. "The natives are getting restless."

"I'll have to stay here and wait for the crime scene crew." Joe grabbed the door handle and firmly pulled the door shut. "We may have more questions for you later," he warned them both.

The ambulance was already gone, taking with it the unidentified body. The fire truck was still parked out front and somehow, her grandsons had managed to wheedle their way inside. Ryan was wearing one of the fireman's black helmets. He waved to Gloria from the driver's seat.

She hurried over to get the boys out of there before they wore out their welcome. Gloria thanked the nice men for showing the truck to the boys before corralling them into the car.

On the way back to the house, the boys were talking up a storm. They both decided *they* were going to be firefighters when they grew up.

Andrea was strangely silent.

The boys ran inside the house as Gloria walked Andrea over to her car. "So you think that was the same backpack that was in the barn loft?"

Andrea nodded. "I'm almost 100% positive."

"What about the house? Do you still want it even after finding a dead body?"

Her head bobbed up and down. "Yes, I just love that house."

"Promise me you'll have some contractors take a look at it before you sign any contract. I'd hate to see you get saddled with a money pit."

Andrea nodded absentmindedly as she got into her car. Gloria had a feeling no matter how much the repairs were going to cost – Andrea had every intention of buying the place.

Back in the kitchen, the boys were rummaging around the cupboards. "We're hungry," Ryan whined.

It had been a long day and Gloria was in no mood to cook. "How 'bout I take you down to Dot's for dinner?" Dot's Kitchen was the only restaurant in their small town of Belhaven and it was owned by one of Gloria's closest friends, Dorothy Jenkins.

The boys ran over to the door. Tyler yanked the door wide open. "Can we go now?"

Gloria grabbed her purse and the threesome headed back out. Gloria eased Annabelle into an open spot, making sure she left enough room on the passenger side so the boys wouldn't smack the door into the car beside them.

The place was busy but the three managed to find an open booth near the front.

Dot spied them right away. She made her way over to where they had just settled in. "Everyone's talking about the body you found this afternoon at the old Johnson mansion." Gloria scooched over so Dot could slide in beside her.

Gloria shook her head. It never ceased to amaze her how quickly news spread in this little town.

Dot was curious. "Which one of you found the body?"

Tyler piped up. "Andrea did. Out in the shed," he added.

Gloria was just about to say they didn't really get a look at the body when Ruth caught sight of them. She shooed the boys over before squeezing in beside them. "You found a body over at the old place on the hill?"

Gloria nodded. "We didn't really see anything. The body was covered with a tarp. The only thing sticking out was a hand. As soon as we saw that, we shut the door and called the police," she explained. "By the time they loaded it in the ambulance, it was completely covered."

Ruth shook her head. "I knew I should've gone with you two."

"Well, I'm glad I wasn't there," Dot declared. She glanced over at the boys. "Did they see it too?"

"No, Grams covered my eyes and she wouldn't let Ryan even close to the shed." Tyler ripped open a packet of sugar, tipped his head back and emptied the contents into his mouth. "We're hungry."

Dot stood up. She'd completely forgotten about taking their order. "I'm sorry, Tyler. With all the excitement, I forgot all about food."

Dot jotted down their orders and walked away but Ruth didn't budge. "So what does the inside of the old place look like?"

Ryan reached for a packet of sugar. "It's really cool. It has secret rooms and everything."

Gloria nodded. "The inside of the house is in much better condition than the outside. Andrea just loved it. Wouldn't be surprised if she bought it."

Ruth eventually ran out of questions and finally left them alone. That didn't last long. It seemed like everyone in the small town had already heard about the body and more than half a dozen town folk came over to ask Gloria and the boys about it.

Dot finally made her way back to their booth, balancing a tray loaded with dinner plates. She dropped three large, greasy burgers and a pile of crispy French fries on the table. Tyler took a huge bite of the burger. "We're famouth Grams," he declared.

Lucy wandered in a few minutes later. She spotted them as soon as she stepped in the door. Gloria made room next to her as Lucy plopped down. "What is it with you and dead bodies?"

"More like Andrea and me and dead bodies." Gloria observed.

"Well, I won't bother asking you a million questions. I've already heard Andrea found the body, the boys didn't see anything and there was a navy blue backpack next to the body."

Lucy lowered her voice and glanced around. "Do you think it's the same one that was in your barn?"

Gloria took a sip of Diet Coke and nodded. "Yeah, Andrea's almost positive it's the same one..."

"So the dead man was in your barn?" Lucy shook her head. The mystery was getting more frightening by the minute.

Gloria was at a loss. "I don't know what to think. Hopefully, we can find out who the poor man was and maybe shed some light on it all."

Lucy made a keen observation. "Looks like you got another mystery on your hands..."

And she certainly did. The wheels were already spinning in Gloria's head but there wasn't much to go on until they found out who the person was.

By the time Jill and Greg made it to the farm later that evening, it was already dark. The boys were sad to be leaving. "Can we come back next weekend?" Ryan pleaded.

"No, I'm sure Grams is going to need a good month to recuperate from this visit," Jill said firmly.

Gloria wrapped the boys in one final hug before watching them leave. She slowly closed the door behind them. The house was eerily quiet. She glanced up at the kitchen clock. Jill would probably be calling in oh, about half an hour. After the boys filled her in on dead bodies, Tyler swinging from the loft, people sneaking into her barn in the middle of the night...

Her prediction wasn't far off. It took approximately 22 minutes for her phone to ring. "Hi Jill." No need in pretending she didn't know who was calling.

Her daughter was nearly hysterical. "What is going on over there? Did you really find a dead body? Was there someone in your barn? Did you ever find the snake?"

"Jill, everything is fine. I'm safe." The next part might not help but it was worth a try. "We think the person that was in my barn is the same one we found dead out at the Johnson place."

"Oh my gosh! I don't even know what to say!" Jill wasn't done. "We're on our way back over there to pick you up. You aren't staying in that house for one more hour!"

This was exactly what Gloria was afraid would happen. "Jill. I'm not going anywhere. This is my home," she calmly but firmly replied.

"Fine, then I'm buying you a German Shepard. And a gun," she added.

"Puddles oughta love that!" The thought actually made her smile. Puddles would freak out if Gloria got a dog.

Gloria glanced down. Puddles was rolling around on the kitchen floor, reclaiming his territory. She rubbed his belly with her foot, a sure sign of attack as he playfully began biting her foot and lightly clawing her heel.

It took another ten minutes before Jill calmed down enough to promise not to drive back over to her mother's house that very instant. Gloria glanced at the phone in her hand before setting it back in the cradle. She shook her head, certain that she hadn't heard the last of it.

After checking to make sure the doors were locked, she wearily tromped off to the bathroom.

Yes, those grandsons of hers really had worn her out.

Chapter 3

Gloria woke the next morning to the sound of a light tap-tap on her window. She pried open an eye and glanced at the clock. It was 7:30 in the morning. So much for sleeping in.

She crawled from her warm bed and made her way over to the bedroom window. She lifted the shade just a tad. Just enough to see Jill's eyeball peering in at her from the other side of the sill. Gloria motioned her around to the front.

By the time she got to the kitchen, Jill was already standing at the door and she wasn't alone. Beside her was a peppy looking pup. Well, maybe not a quite a pup.

Gloria looked down at the panting dog. "Who's this?"

"This is Mallory. Mally for short. She's a Springer Spaniel." Jill stuck the leash in Gloria's hand. "Congratulations! She's all yours."

Gloria looked down at the leash still attached to the dog. "But I don't want a dog." Her voice sounded whiny, even to herself. Or maybe it was borderline panic. "Puddles will be terrified," she argued.

She could've sworn the poor dog's face fell when she heard that. Gloria bent down and patted her head. "I'm sorry girl. You're such a beautiful dog." And she was beautiful. Covered in soft, snow white fur with large patches of shiny brown that looked like warm chocolate. Soulful brown eyes gazed pleadingly up at her.

"If you don't keep her, I'll have to take her back to the shelter," Jill threatened.

Gloria couldn't let that happen. She quickly caved. After all, she didn't want to break the poor dog's heart. "Well, maybe we can keep her for a trial run."

That was all Jill needed to hear. There was no way she was going to give her mother a chance to change her mind. "Look, I gotta run." She pointed to the side of the house. "There's a big bag of dog food over here. She eats twice a day."

Jill paused at the bottom step. "Oh, and she absolutely loves corn on the cob." She started laughing as Mally looked at her with pleading eyes as if to say, "Don't tell all my secrets."

"She chews the corn off and then gnaws on the cob like it's a bone."

Gloria slowly shut the door as she looked down at her new companion. "Let me go find Puddles. You two need to sort this out real quick."

It was too late. Puddles was already in the kitchen, creeping across the floor as he inched his way towards the interloper. Mally dropped on all fours and scooted forward, her nails scraping the vinyl floor as she pulled herself along. Gloria held her breath as the two slowly sniffed each other.

Without warning, Puddles butted his head across the side of Mally's face and began purring. Gloria stuck a hand on her hip as she shook her head. Miracles never ceased. The two actually liked each other. "Well, it would appear to me that I now have two critters to keep me company."

They both looked up at her in adoration as if they understood what she was saying. Maybe this dog thing wasn't such a bad idea after all.

Gloria poured a pot of cold water into the coffee machine before rambling off to the bathroom to get ready for her day. If she wasn't busy before, a dog and new murder investigation would most definitely fill up her days.

A brilliant thought occurred to her as warm water cascaded over her weary body. Weren't Springer Spaniels good hunting dogs? Surely they have some sort of extraordinary sniffers that would be useful when searching for clues.

Gloria smiled to herself. Mally would be earning her keep and she was going to start by putting her to work right there on the farm – and she could start in the barn!

A loud bark interrupted her thoughts. She quickly grabbed a towel and made a dash for the kitchen. Visions of Puddles, or what was left of Puddles, swam before her eyes – nothing but a loose pile of furball floating around on the kitchen floor after Mally chewed him up and spit him out.

73

Alas, that was not the sight that greeted her. The two were wrestling around on the floor nipping at each other and having a grand old time.

Gloria clutched the towel around her. "*Ahem.*" The action stopped. The two of them stared up at her, guilt written all over their furry faces. "If I didn't know better, I'd think the two of you were somehow related."

Gloria quickly finished dressing before pouring a cup of coffee and plopping down at the table. A sad, pitiful face was staring right at her. Not blinking. She sighed deeply. Until she could get this dog-thing figured out, she'd just have to guess as to what the look was for. "Do you need to go outside?"

Mally sprang to her feet and made a beeline for the kitchen door, skidding to a sudden halt as she crashed into the glass pane. She obviously knew what that meant and she most definitely wanted to go outside. She whine pathetically as she pawed at the door.

Gloria grabbed the leash, firmly attached it to Mally's red collar and headed outside. The morning was cool and damp. Heavy clouds threatened to let loose some serious rain. She shivered. It was too late to go back in and grab a jacket. The energetic mutt was ready to explore.

Mally sniffed her way over to the garden, pausing long enough to examine a nearby tree and deeming it the perfect spot to mark her territory.

They took a quick tromp through the garden. Thank goodness there was nothing left to trample except for a few mushy pumpkins and rotting tomatoes that never made it out alive. Next, they moved on to the barn. With a burst of energy Gloria hadn't experienced since the grandkids left less than 24 hours ago, Mally started trotting along. This was apparently some sort of test to see if Gloria could keep up because the trot soon became a full out run. By the time they reached the barn, Gloria's yard shoes were long gone, abandoned halfway between the gravel drive and the barn door.

Gloria plucked the hidden key from above the door frame and unlocked the shiny new padlock. The door was open mere inches before Mally managed to wiggle her way inside. She stood motionless for a second, as if overwhelmed by all the new smells and sights around her.

It didn't take long for curiosity to get the best of her as she yanked Gloria across the barn floor towards the milking parlor. With the thoroughness of a Bloodhound, the dog investigated every single stall, sniffing posts, piles of straw and anything else Gloria would let her get close enough to. After that, they worked their way back out to the main barn area.

A perimeter sniff was now in order. Much to Gloria's relief, the dog gave an all-clear when she decided there wasn't anything left in the barn to hold her interest.

Gloria locked the barn and headed in the direction of her missing shoes. Mally suddenly let out a low growl followed by a loud bark. It wasn't a "Hey, I'm glad you have your shoes back bark." More like a warning bark. Gloria slipped her shoes back on and looked up just in time to see a four door sedan with tinted windows roll into the drive.

Mally yanked Gloria forward in the direction of the unfamiliar vehicle. "You have GOT to stop doing that before you jerk my arm right out of its socket!" she scolded. The dog almost had the sense to look guilty but she was way more curious about who was in the drive.

The car was one Gloria didn't recognize but the person that emerged definitely was. Officer Kennedy made his way over to where the two were waiting. He bent down to let Mally sniff his hand. "Who do we have here?"

"My lovely daughter heard someone was wandering around outside the other night and decided I needed a guard dog."

Kennedy got the seal of approval as Mally slurped at his hand and wagged her tail vigorously. "She's a beauty."

Gloria could've sworn the crazy dog smiled at his compliment as she circled him, wrapping herself and her rope around his legs.

Gloria quickly grabbed the leash and freed the man. "Sorry about that!"

"She's fine. I have a Golden Retriever myself. Looks like they're about the same age. Lots of energy!"

She shook her head. "You can say that again."

He quickly changed the subject. "What is it with you and dead bodies?" He was leaning against his car now, arms crossed as he studied the woman in front of him.

"We didn't plan on finding a dead body. It just happened," she confessed.

"Ever heard of Walking Stan?"

Gloria nodded. "Everyone in Belhaven knows Walking Stan."

Walking Stan was a bit of an odd duck. He'd lived in Belhaven for as long as Gloria could remember, right out on the edge of town in a purple house. Actually, just around the corner from Gloria's farm. He was pretty much a loner. Rumor had it he was filthy rich but you'd never know it by looking at him – or his house. He was a scrawny little man with long, shaggy hair. He drove a beat up old van that seemed to break down every other day. Odd thing about Walking Stan was, you would see his van on the side of the road, hood up as if the engine just conked out. A short distance away, he'd be thumbing a ride to wherever. Hours later, the van would be gone from the side of the road and more often than not, could be found sitting in his driveway, right next to the purple house. Folks said he was so cheap, he'd pretend to have engine trouble just so he could catch a free ride and save on gas.

He wasn't really scary and most people didn't mind giving him a lift if they were going in the same direction. He was a man of few words, though. No one really knew where he came from or if he even had any family.

"The dead man you found in the shed is Walking Stan's brother."

You could've knocked Gloria over with a feather. "He had a brother?"

He nodded. "His name was Arthur Blackstone."

Gloria was speechless. All she could do was shake her head. She wasn't sure if she'd ever even heard what Walking Stan's last name was.

Officer Kennedy wasn't done. "They found a backpack near his body. A navy blue one."

She nodded at that. "We didn't get a look at the man in the shed since he was covered in a tarp and all. The only thing sticking out was a hand. We got a quick look at the backpack before the police took it away."

Kennedy was curious. "Did it look familiar?"

Gloria nodded. "Andrea said it looked like the one she saw in my loft a couple weeks ago."

Kennedy shook his head. None of this was adding up. If this Arthur fellow was Walking Stan's brother, why was he hiding out in Gloria's barn?

"What was in the backpack?" Gloria was hoping for some sort of clue.

"It was empty, all except for a small piece of paper with Walking Stan's address on it." He went on. "We paid a visit to Stan. That's when he told us it was his brother. Said Arthur showed up on his doorstep out of the blue."

He absentmindedly bent down to stroke Mally's head. "A very odd man. Not much of a talker."

"Yeah, that's him for sure." Gloria nodded. "So did you check the Johnson house?"

He nodded. "Clean. Not a single clue."

Gloria opened her mouth to speak and then quickly closed it. She was torn. Should she mention what she discovered at the house the other day? After all, she didn't want him thinking she was already working "the case." She decided to take her chances since she really wanted his thoughts. "I noticed something when we were in the house the other day..."

Kennedy waited. This is what he had been hoping for. He hated to admit it but this woman was a stickler for details. She knew something.

"It was the kitchen. The kitchen in that house was really clean. You know, not dusty like it hadn't been lived in for years," she explained.

That in itself might not be earth shattering clue material but what she said next, well that might be something. "And when I turned on the kitchen faucet, the water was clear. If the well and the pipes hadn't been used for years, wouldn't the water have rust in it?"

Kennedy nodded thoughtfully. Hmmm, so maybe there were more clues inside the house.... "Is that all?"

She nodded sheepishly. "Yeah, that's it."

Kennedy looked at his watch. "I'm off duty now. If you've got the time, maybe I can take you up on that offer for a cup of coffee..."

The blood instantly drained from Gloria's face before returning with a vengeance and causing it to turn the brightest shade of pink. Her tongue turned traitor as it twisted up in her mouth. The only thing that came out was a pathetic, squeaky "Of course." She whirled around, hoping he hadn't noticed the color of her face and praying he wouldn't change his mind.

Her fingers were slicker than a can of Crisco as she fumbled with the cups, almost dumped a plate of cookies on the floor and then nearly tripped over the darned cat who decided it was time to check out the visitor.

The man was obviously an animal lover because Puddles jumped up on his lap and started purring loudly. "How many pets do you have?"

Gloria breathed a sigh of relief when everything was safely on the table and she was able to sit down. "Just two. Probably two too many, though."

She looked at Mally warningly. "She's on probation. I haven't decided if I'll keep her." But she knew that wasn't true. The dog was here to stay.

Mally dropped to the floor and laid her head on top of her paws, staring at Gloria remorsefully. "I'm just kidding. Of course, you're staying."

Paul Kennedy was an expert at putting people at ease and it worked like a charm on the nervous woman across the table. They chatted easily about living in a small town and how much he liked being a cop, even though he didn't patrol the streets very often anymore.

He leaned back in the chair. "I'm thinking about retiring in the next couple years." He stared blankly out the window. "My wife died a few years back. Just not sure what I'll do with myself if I don't have a job to go to every day."

Gloria stared down at her hands. So they were both in the same boat... "Same here. My husband James passed away a couple years ago. He had a heart attack in his sleep." She started to tear up as she spoke the words. "At least he died peacefully..."

Kennedy reached over and gently squeezed her hand. "I'm sorry. I didn't mean to upset you."

She shook her head. "It's OK." A sigh escaped her lips. "It just gets lonely sometimes."

Paul felt a kindred spirit with the woman seated across from him. "Maybe I could take you to dinner one evening?" he asked hopefully.

Gloria's head shot up, a look of surprise spread across her face. "That would be lovely." She surprised herself with how quickly she answered. "I would like that very much."

Kennedy eased out of the chair and reluctantly stood. "How does Friday night sound?"

It sounded fabulous to Gloria. She nodded.

"Good, I'll pick you up around 6 then?"

She nodded again, too nervous to answer.

The dog followed them to the door. No way were *they* going to go outside without her!

By the time Gloria and Mally made their way back inside, Gloria's phone was ringing. It was Ruth. "Do you know who the dead guy in the shed was?"

"Yep."

Ruth was like a deflated balloon. "You do?"

85

"Mmhm. It was Walking Stan's brother, Arthur."

"I'd like to know how you keep finding this stuff out before me," she huffed.

A small smile played across Gloria's lips. There was no way she was going to tell her that Paul Kennedy was just at her house. That would really start the tongues in Belhaven wagging. "Look, I gotta run. The dog needs to go out," she fibbed.

"What dog?" But Gloria had already hung up. She smiled into the phone knowing that right about now Ruth was annoyed as all get out.

The phone was ringing again. Gloria sighed tiredly. Careful what you wish for. First she was bored to death and now she couldn't even sit down.

"Hello?"

"How's Mally doing?" It was Jill.

"We're having a grand old time. We've already tromped through the garden and thoroughly investigated the big red barn."

"Did she find anything?"

"You mean like clues as to who was in the barn the other night?" Gloria asked innocently.

"Yeah. That!"

Gloria poured another cup of coffee and sat down. This might take awhile. "No, but I don't think that's going to be a problem anymore."

"Oh, really. Why is that?"

Because the person who was in my barn is the same one we found dead out at the old Johnson place."

Jill was completely confused. "H-how on earth do you know that?"

"Officer Kennedy stopped by a few minutes ago. He told me the man was Walking Stan's brother." Gloria held her breath, waiting for her daughter to react.

"Who is Officer Kennedy?"

Gloria sighed. "It's a long story. He's with the Montbay Sheriff Department."

"He?"

"Yep."

Jill sounded aggravated. "I give up! You have people hiding in your barn that turn up dead and now cops are stopping by your house for a visit. Next you'll tell me you're going on a date!"

Gloria smiled. "Friday night."

"Ugh! I'm not saying anything else. Who knows what else I'm going to find out."

Jill paused before continuing her rant. What her mom wasn't saying was way more telling than what she was. She sounded excited, like maybe she was interested in this Kennedy fellow.

Jill switched gears. "What are you going to wear?"

Wear? Oh, my. Gloria hadn't even gotten that far yet. Now she was going to have to worry about what to wear??

"I'll stop by later this week and help you pick something out. Something young and sexy." Jill added.

Gloria blushed. "Stop that!"

Jill suddenly began yelling. "Look, I gotta go. The boys are at it again!"

The line went dead. Gloria shook her head. Better her than me.

The rest of the afternoon was peaceful and quiet. It was out on the porch later that evening that Gloria discovered Mally was content to curl up at her feet and take a dog nap. There was one small problem, though. The pooch considered squirrels to be big game. Every time lifted her head and spotted one, she sprinted down the steps and peeled across the lawn as if her tail were on fire. Gloria couldn't fault her that one little flaw. Otherwise, she was pretty darn perfect.

They stayed on the porch for a long time. Gloria's stomach growled. She glanced at her watch. "You hungry yet, Mally?" Her ears perked up when she realized food was being discussed. She wandered over to the door and patiently waited for Gloria to open it.

Minutes later, leftover slices of meatloaf tantalized the hungry pup's nose as her sniffer found its way over to the edge of the kitchen counter. Gloria glanced down at the dog who was now directly under foot. "I bet you like meatloaf."

She pulled a paper plate from the cupboard. She sliced several thin pieces and arranged them on the plate before setting the plate on the floor. Gloria grabbed her own plate and headed for the living room, eager to see if the evening news had any updates on Arthur's murder.

She no more than sat down in her comfy recliner when Mally sidled up next to Gloria, carrying the empty paper plate in her mouth. "Well, look at that. I guess that means you want more, huh."

She dropped a few more small pieces on the plate as Puddles jumped up and wiggled in next to Gloria. "Between the two of you, I won't have anything to eat myself," she grumbled. But she didn't really mean it. She let Puddles eat a few pieces out of her hand before finishing what was left.

The news was just starting. Unfortunately, there was no mention of the murder. It looked as if she'd have to work on getting more clues on her own. What better place to start than with Walking Stan himself – if she could get him to talk, that is. Tomorrow would be the perfect time to try.

Chapter 4

First thing the next morning Gloria made a list of questions she wanted to ask Walking Stan. After all, how much sense would it make to show up on his doorstep if she had no idea what she wanted to say?

She grabbed her car keys and purse and headed for the door. Mally was already waiting for her, stuffed toy firmly clenched in her mouth. "Where do you think you're going?"

She pawed at the door lightly. A small, pitiful whine escaped. "You can go this time. Just don't think that you're going to go *every time,* got that?" Gloria tried to sound stern but even to her own ears it rang hollow. They all knew who was running the show these days and it definitely wasn't Gloria.

It took less than a minute for Gloria to turn onto the road where the only purple house in Belhaven could be found. Or it used to be purple. Hard telling what it looked like now. She cautiously pulled into the drive. The house was still purple but more of a lilac color from years of fading in the sun. She turned the car off and glanced warily at the large picture window in front. The shades were drawn tight. The van was in the drive so Stan was either in the house or managed to hitch a ride to who-knows-where.

She grabbed the handle. Mally dropped her stuffed animal on the seat and squeezed in next to Gloria. "You stay here," she commanded. Sad, mournful eyes met hers but it wasn't going to work this time. She was going to have to stay put for a few minutes.

The cement steps leading to the front door were in need of some serious repair. Gloria sidestepped the crumbling corners as she made her way to the front door. Before she could change her mind, she firmly pressed the doorbell and nervously waited.

The door creaked open, just a teeny bit. One hazel colored eyeball stared through the crack. "Who is it?"

The hair on the back of Gloria's neck rose unexpectedly. She swallowed hard. "G-Gloria

Rutherford," she stammered. "Your neighbor down the road." She closed her eyes and prayed he wouldn't fling the door open, shotgun in hand. Thankfully, he did open the door and there wasn't a gun. Just a metal baseball bat. Of course, that would hurt pretty badly, but not nearly as much as being shot.

A small disheveled man stood in the doorway. He eyed her suspiciously. "Yeah, what do you want?"

So much for pleasantries. "I-uh, just wanted to tell you that I'm sorry about your brother..."

The old man shook a shaggy head. "He wasn't much of kinfolk to me. Nothin' but a thief and a crook."

Jackpot! So the brother was a criminal...

"Why do you say he was a crook?"

Walking Stan didn't answer. Instead, a scarred hand that reminded her of a claw waved her inside. She hesitated for a fraction of a second before taking a deep breath and following him in.

She glanced back at Mally whose snout was smashed against the driver side glass window. Hopefully, she'd make it back out alive.

The inside of the house was surprisingly tidy. Almost too tidy for a known recluse and confirmed bachelor. The walls were painted a normal shade of light beige. No, the inside definitely did not match the outside.

"You have a nice little place here, Mr. Stan."

He swung around and studied her for a moment, as if he thought she was making fun of him and his house. "Mr. Blackstone. But you can call me Stan." A toothy grin accompanied the words.

He likes me! Oh no! I hope he doesn't like me like that or think that I'm trying to hit on him. The thought hadn't occurred to Gloria until that precise moment. She took a small step back.

It was time to steer the conversation back to the reason for her visit. "So why do you think your brother is a crook?"

He reached over and plucked a newspaper clipping off the end table. He handed it to Gloria. "This is my brother."

She snatched her reading glasses from inside her purse and slipped them on. The article was about six months old and briefly described a bank robbery in Grand Rapids. She quickly scanned the short story. The robber was never apprehended.

Gloria handed the news article back to Stan. "And you're sure the robber was your brother?"

Stan nodded solemnly. "I know it for a fact. Came by here a few months ago asking me if he could crash on my couch. He had a backpack full of cash with him. That's when he told me he was the one that robbed the bank."

He carefully set the piece of paper back on the stand. "Told him I don't take kindly to thieves and that he best be leaving before I called the police on him."

"That was the last you heard of him?"

He shook his head. "It was up until a few days ago. He was back on my doorstep lookin' real scared. Said he owed a lot of money - gambling debts - to some real bad people and wanted me to hang onto what money he had left from the robbery."

Stan raised his hands in front of him. "Told him I wanted nothin' to do with it and he better leave."

"So he did?" she prompted.

Stan nodded. "Yep, that's the last I heard of him 'til the other day when the officer came 'round and told me they'd found him dead in the back shed of that big old house on the hill."

He scratched his scruffy beard thoughtfully. "Looks like the folks that were after him finally tracked him down."

"Your brother never gave you any clue as to who might be after him?"

He shook his head. "Nope, none at all..."

Gloria was curious. "Did you tell the police about the money?"

"Nope. I sure didn't. They didn't ask if I knew what was in the backpack and I didn't offer. No sense in stirring up a hornets nest. My brother's dead and the killers are looong gone."

Gloria took another step back and reached behind her, groping for the door handle. "Well, I'm sorry about your brother. I hope for your sake you're right and the killers are long gone."

Stan seemed pretty confident. "But if not," he grabbed his metal bat and tapped it against the gnarled hand, "they'll be sorry if they come around here and try to mess with Stanley Blackstone. You can be sure of that."

Gloria heaved a sigh of relief as she stepped out the door and back onto the porch. She glanced at Mally who was sitting in the exact same spot that Gloria left her.

Stan peeked his head around the corner of the door. "Pretty dog."

Gloria couldn't agree more. "Yeah, she's a keeper, that's for sure."

She pulled the car door open before turning back. Stan was standing in the doorway watching her. "Maybe you should get a dog, Stan. They're good company and you could probably use a good watchdog."

He scratched his beard as he studied the dog thoughtfully. "Yeah, been thinkin' 'bout it."

That was the end of the conversation as he slipped back inside and silently shut the door behind him.

Gloria scooted Mally over to the passenger side as she hopped in the car. "Were you worried about me, girl?"

Mally took one long, wet swipe at the side of Gloria's face with her tongue. "I swear you're half human." Another lick on the face was her only response as Gloria backed the car out of the driveway.

Today was errand day and the next stop was the post office. This time she let Mally get out with her. The dog was as good as gold. She stayed right by Gloria's side as they made their way into the small brick building.

Ruth stepped out from behind the counter when she saw them come in. She reached down and patted Mally's head. "I thought you were kidding about the dog."

"Nope. Jill dropped her off yesterday morning."

Ruth wandered behind the counter and grabbed a dog biscuit from the zip-lock bag inside the top drawer. Mally promptly licked her hand, grabbed the treat and took it to the corner to munch on.

Gloria popped her mail in the slot and turned back to Ruth. "Have you heard how Arthur Blackstone died?"

"Yeah, he was poisoned." Ruth shook her head and tsk-tsked. "Terrible way to die." She was back behind the counter now. "So when is our next Garden Girls meeting? Looks like we have another mysterious murder to discuss."

The last couple weeks had been really busy. The Garden Girls Club hadn't had a chance to get together. Gloria shrugged.

"How 'bout Friday night? We can have dinner together and hold the meeting afterwards."

Gloria shook her head. "That isn't going to work for me." She snapped her fingers at Mally. "C'mon girl. Time to go." Gloria reached for the door handle. "I have a dinner date Friday night." She grinned as she caught a glimpse of Ruth's priceless expression in the reflection of the glass door.

Mally took her place in the passenger side as Gloria started the car. She tapped her fingers on the steering wheel as she hummed along to a catchy Christian tune on the radio.

Her last stop was her best friend Lucy's house. She figured she better stop by and tell Lucy about her date Friday night before Ruth got to her.

It was too late. Lucy met her on the sidewalk, a fist firmly planted on her hip. "How come you didn't tell me you have a date?" she demanded.

She looked down at Mally. "And that you got a dog?" Mally padded over and rubbed up against Lucy. "Is there anything else I don't know? Like you're moving to Dreamwood after all?"

Dreamwood was a retirement home in nearby Green Springs. Gloria's sister Liz lived there and Gloria's daughter, Jill, had been trying for years to get her mom to move there. Gloria had no intention of doing any such thing. The place was sin city. All kinds of shenanigans going on amongst the male and female residents that lived there.

"Absolutely not! I just got the dog and the date. I ran into Ruth when I was at the post office. That's how she found out."

"Hmm." Lucy still wasn't totally convinced.

"Can I come inside or are you mad at me?"

Lucy softened as she waved her friend in. She looked down at Mally. "You can come, too."

Lucy plopped a piece of strawberry pie and tall glass of iced tea in front of Gloria as Mally crawled under the kitchen table, hoping a wayward scrap would fall her way.

"I stopped by Walking Stan's today." Gloria took a bite of freshly glazed strawberry.

Lucy shook her mop of bright red curls. *Oh no. Here we go again. Gloria was definitely working another case.*

"He told me his brother robbed a bank a few months back and that some people were after him. Next thing you know. Bam! He's dead."

"Do the police know that?"

Gloria shook her head. "Nope. He never mentioned it to them."

Lucy drummed freshly polished pink nails on the kitchen table. "Are you going to?"

Gloria took another bite. "You know, his house was almost immaculate on the inside. Very clean and tidy."

"You went inside his house?" Lucy paused. "It was?"

Gloria nodded. "He's actually a very decent man."

"So now what?"

Gloria shook her head. The answer should be obvious. "We have to find out who the killer – or killers – are. I need to get back inside that house."

Gloria was all over the place, jumping from one thing to the next. Lucy was totally confused. "What house?"

"You know, the Johnson mansion. So we can search for more clues." Gloria broke off a small piece of pie crust and shoved it under the table. "Want to go with me?"

"Yeah, I guess I better." She needed to make sure Gloria stayed out of trouble. "I can do it today. Tomorrow is booked up." Lucy reached behind her and plucked a flyer from a small stack of papers on the edge of the counter. She pushed it towards Gloria. "I'm going to start tanning."

Gloria grabbed her reading glasses. "Hmm. Seven Day Cruise to the Southern Caribbean."

She looked up at Lucy. "You won?" Gloria was never good at those stupid contests. She never won anything.

Lucy shook her head. "Not yet but I'm going to. It's called using the power of positive thinking."

Gloria shook her head as she grabbed her cellphone and dialed Andrea's number. As luck would have it, Andrea had a contractor already at the house working on an estimate.

Gloria jumped to her feet. "C'mon. Let's go!"

She slowly pulled Annabelle in the drive, past the rusty old gate and parked directly behind the contractor's van. The house looked even more sinister than it had the last time they were there. Murder sure did have a way of casting a dark shadow over everything.

The first place Gloria wanted to check out was the shed. She poked around under the canvas, behind a small stack of clay pots and under the worn, wooden shelf. There was nothing. Not a single clue to be found.

Lucy peeked around Gloria's shoulder. "Is this where you found the body?"

Gloria nodded in disappointment. Hopefully this trip wouldn't turn out to be a complete waste of time!

The girls waved at the man who was measuring the outside of the house. Lucy followed Gloria inside the front entrance. They stopped just inside as Lucy glanced around the grand hall in awe. She loved old, historic architecture and this place oozed of it.

Gloria prodded her along. "Let's check out the kitchen." There was no time to dilly dally looking around. They were on a mission!

She marched into the kitchen and then abruptly stopped. There just had to be some sort of clue. Someone had been in here. Either the victim or the killer...

Her sharp eyes slowly surveyed the counters, the cabinets. One-by-one she opened the cupboards and peered inside.   They were all empty. All of them except for the very last one on the end. Something was wedged against the side of the wooden frame.

Lucy walked over to stand beside Gloria. "What is that?"

Good question. *What was it?*

Gloria picked it up and flipped it over. It was a hotel door card. *Green Springs Inn.*

"It's exactly what I was looking for. A clue."

They thoroughly searched the rest of the kitchen but came up empty-handed.

The girls made their way back to the car. Gloria slipped into the driver seat and dropped the key card into her purse. She turned to her friend. "You have time to make a quick trip to Green Springs?"

Green Springs Inn was a small mom-n-pop motel. The white, one-story structure took up half a city block. Gloria pulled in an empty parking spot directly in front of the office. She and Lucy made their way inside the front door. They rang the silver bell sitting on top of the faded green Formica countertop. A small, dark-haired woman suddenly appeared. "Can I help you?"

Gloria set the room card on the counter. "We found this card. We were wondering...is there any way to scan the card and find out who might have stayed in your hotel using this card and the date they were here?"

The woman turned the card over in her hand. "This is definitely ours."

She swiped the card through the machine behind the counter. "From what I can tell, this was the only card that was issued and the guest stayed two nights. The person checked out a week ago."

The clerk handed the card back as she eyed them suspiciously. The two women *looked* like a couple nice ladies. "For privacy reasons, I can't tell you the guest's name."

Gloria was disappointed. There had to be some way around this. Hmmm. "If I gave you the name, maybe you could just nod your head if I got it right?" Gloria asked hopefully.

The clerk tipped her head to one side. She didn't think that would be breaking any company rule. "I suppose so..."

Gloria took a deep breath and blurted out. "Blackstone."

The clerk nodded ever-so-slightly. *Bingo!*

So the key card inside the house belonged to Blackstone. But why would Arthur Blackstone be sleeping in her barn and hiding out at the old Johnson mansion if he had a hotel room in Green Springs? To Gloria, that just didn't make any sense. "You've been very helpful uhhh..."

"Jane. Jane Jackson."

"Thank you, Jane."

They made their way out onto the sidewalk. Lucy quietly closed the door behind them. "Now what?"

"Maybe he ran out of money and had to check out?"

But Walking Stan said he had a backpack full of money. If that was the case, what happened to all that cash? Maybe it was time to pay Stan another visit.

Gloria dropped Lucy off and headed home. She pulled in the drive and glanced in the rearview mirror. Mally was sprawled out in the back seat, sound asleep. "Come on, girl. Time to get out."

Mally's head jerked up. She jumped to her feet and bounded out of the car, racing Gloria to the porch door.

Puddles was waiting just on the other side. Mally gave Puddles a quick lick "hello" and darted over to her empty food dish. She stared back at Gloria with a pathetic "feed me" look. Apparently, all this detective work was making her hungry.

Gloria's brain was in overdrive as she poured food into both Mally and Puddles dishes. Something about the murder case just wasn't adding up. There was a reason Arthur Blackstone was hiding out in Gloria's barn and the Johnson place. He was hiding from someone, but who? Who would know about the robbery and that

Blackstone had a pile of cash? Was there a second bank robber that got stiffed and tracked Blackstone down to get it? Or was it what his brother said? His gambling debts ended up being his downfall.

There was a missing puzzle piece and Gloria was bound and determined to figure it out!

Hungry herself, Gloria threw together a ham and cheese sandwich, heavy on the mayo, tossed some potato chips on the side and plopped down in the kitchen chair. She gazed out the window as she slowly chewed her sandwich.

Was Walking Stan lying? Was he the real killer? She just wasn't getting the vibe that he was the killer. It was quite possible he was hiding something, though.

Her ringing telephone dragged her from deep thought.

"Hello?"

"Hello, Gloria. It's Paul. Paul Kennedy." He paused. "Just calling to remind you of our date Friday night."

Gloria blushed. Good thing he wasn't right in front of her. "Yes, I'm really looking forward to it."

"Have you found anything else out about the Blackstone murder?" He knew darned well she'd been sniffing around and probably turned up something else.

Instead of answering right away, she turned it right back on him. "Have you?"

He smiled into the phone. "Possibly. You tell me what you found out and I'll tell you what I know."

That sounded fair enough. "The backpack in the shed – the same one Andrea saw in my garage. It belonged to Arthur Blackstone. According to his brother Stan, it was full of cash."

"Stan Blackstone told you that?" Kennedy asked incredulously.

"Yeah. The other day when I dropped by there."

Interesting. Blackstone didn't share that tidbit with him when he paid a visit...

"That's not all. He said his brother got the money from robbing a bank a few months back and that someone was after the money but he didn't say who."

Kennedy was thinking out loud. "I wonder why he didn't think that information would be important to the investigation. Or maybe he's trying to hide something."

Gloria nodded. "I have a hunch there's more to the story than meets the eye."

She was just about to mention the hotel but stopped short. She needed to do a little more digging around before sharing that tidbit.

It was his turn to help her out. "So what do you know?"

"Arthur Blackstone was poisoned."

Gloria was disappointed. She already knew that!

Paul finished by saying that's all he had on the case as of right now. He thanked her for telling him about the cash. At least now there was a motive for murder. "See you Friday night then?"

"Yes, of course. Paul." Might as well start calling him by his first name. After all, he was calling her by her first name.

Chapter 5

Stan Blackstone answered his door on the first ring. "You again."

Gloria ignored the sarcasm. Maybe he wasn't such a great guy after all. "Did you know your brother checked in to the Green Springs Inn shortly before his death?"

A stony expression settled on Walking Stan's face. If this piece of news was a surprise to him, he didn't let on. "You ought not be snooping around in something that's none of your business," he warned.

"Aren't you the least bit concerned about finding your brother's killer?"

"Stay out of it!" The door slammed in Gloria's face before she could say anything else.

Disappointed with the results of her visit and certain she had now ticked off the only person who might have more information on Arthur Blackstone's killer, Gloria slowly made her way back to the car.

Her investigation was at a standstill and she was more than a little perturbed. Maybe Ruth had more info.

She strolled into the post office and walked right up to the counter, not bothering to hide the fact that the only reason she was in the post office was to pump Ruth for any new information on the murder.

Gloria leaned on the counter and gazed at her friend. "Hear any new gossip about Arthur Blackstone's murder?"

Ruth looked around before leaning forward. "Yeah. He had a gambling debt that finally caught up with him," she whispered.

Gloria already knew that much. She didn't have the heart to tell Ruth. "Is that it?"

"Yeah. There just aren't that many people talking. It's all rather mysterious." Ruth glanced over Gloria's head before continuing. "Heck, a week ago, we didn't even know Walking Stan had a brother."

That was true. And the fact that the entire family kept to themselves. There just wasn't much to go on.

Gloria slowly started Annabelle and pulled back onto the small, two lane street. She got the nagging feeling that she was missing a major clue and that clue was hidden somewhere in the old house on the hill.

She let Mally out the back door to romp around the yard and chase a few squirrels before she called Lucy. "Are you ready for a stakeout?"

"When? Bill and I are going skydiving this afternoon."

"Lucy, you're going to give yourself a heart attack. You're not a spring chicken anymore."

"I'd rather die doing something like that than have someone stab me to death over a cheating spouse or poison me over some stolen cash!" Lucy argued.

Good point. "True. What time will you be back?"

"After dinner."

"Great! I'll pick you up around 8 tonight!" Gloria's heart pounded at the thought of a covert night time investigation. "Oh, and wear dark clothes."

She quickly hung up before Lucy could change her mind.

The afternoon dragged on as Gloria impatiently waited for nightfall. Finally, it was time to go. Gloria's heart was pounding by the time she made her way up the steps of Lucy's house. She barely had a chance to knock before the door swung open.

Lucy motioned her inside and quickly shut the door. "I have something." She reached over and grabbed a necklace off the table. She dropped it around Gloria's neck.

Gloria looked down. "What's this?"

Lucy had an identical one dangling from her neck. She grabbed the end in her hand and lifted it up. "One of those medical alert thingy's."

Gloria pulled the end closer to her face. "Where on earth did you get these?"

"I picked them up a while ago." Lucy was pretty pleased with herself. "They were buy one, get one free on one of those late night infomercials."

"How's this going to help us if we press the button and help shows up at your house?"

Lucy shook her head. "Nope. This is one of the newer ones with GPS. They can find you no matter where you're at."

Gloria stared at the dangling contraption and shrugged. Hey, who knows. Maybe it really would come in handy.

Gloria parked the car two short blocks from the old house. The girls made their way down the back alley until they were directly behind the old place. Gloria motioned Lucy over to the overgrown shrubbery near the edge of the property. The spooky house loomed in the distance. It was scary in the daytime and even more sinister looking at night. *What if the place really was haunted?*

Lucy parted the greenery as she peered through. "Now what?"

Gloria really didn't have a plan yet. "We wait."

They crouched low in the same position for several long minutes until Lucy got a cramp in her calf. "I gotta sit down."

Gloria glanced down at the dark earth. "Have a seat then. But watch out for snakes," she warned.

Lucy jumped up and swatted at her rear. "Thanks for the warning," she muttered.

Gloria suddenly stood upright. She put a hand on her back, trying to ease her sore muscles. "Time for a closer look."

Lucy stared at her friend incredulously. She was off her rocker. "Are you crazy??"

Maybe Gloria was but there was no one around. Now would be the perfect time to check out the inside without raising any suspicions.

She didn't wait for Lucy as she ducked down and quickly crept toward the looming silhouette. She looked back to see Lucy hovering reluctantly on the back side of the hedge. She waved her over. "Let's go."

Lucy stared up at the black sky wondering what she'd ever done to deserve this. She yanked the knitted cap down over the bright red curls and muttered under her breath, certain this decision probably wasn't going to end well.

The closer they got to the house, the more nervous Gloria got. She stuck a sweaty hand on the front knob and gently twisted. It was locked tight. "We'll need to go around back," she whispered breathlessly.

The double sliders on the back side of the house were locked, too. There was one more door left to try - the one leading into the kitchen. Gloria held her breath as she slowly turned the knob. It easily turned in her hand. She silently pushed the door open and the girls crept inside.

Lucy swallowed nervously. They were definitely breaking the law. Visions of a musty old

121

jail cell and a cellmate named Roxanne came to mind. "Now what?"

Gloria hadn't thought that far ahead. The moon cast a sliver of light inside the kitchen. Just enough to reveal that the room was empty. *What if Blackstone hid the money somewhere inside the house before he was murdered?*

She and Lucy had already thoroughly searched the kitchen the last time they were in the house so no reason to waste any time looking around there.

Gloria made her way through the butler's pantry and into the dining room. She pulled a small flashlight from her pocket and switched it on. A beam of light bounced around the room, casting eerie shadows across the walls.

Lucy clutched her arm. "Someone's going to see the light!" She could almost hear police sirens in the distance.

Gloria shook her head. "No chance. The windows out front are boarded shut. No one can see the light." Unless, of course, it was someone inside the house but no way was she going to point that out to Lucy.

"If you were going to hide money in a big old house like this, where would you put it?" Gloria took a step towards the grand entrance. She stopped in front of the stairway, beaming the flashlight up at the second level.

"Maybe it's in the attic?" Lucy guessed out loud and then wished she hadn't as she shuddered uncontrollably. The last place she wanted to go in the middle of the night in a house that was rumored to be haunted would be the attic. Or the basement. No way was she going to mention it might be in the basement.

Gloria shook her head. "No, that would seem too obvious." She fiddled with the flashlight thoughtfully. "I would hide it in a strategic location. As far away from the exits as possible. Or maybe even somewhere in plain sight." She pointed the flashlight towards the massive living room but quickly dismissed it. "That would be too easy. I think I would hide it upstairs."

Gloria paused when she reached the landing. *Should they go right or left?* Left would take them to the master bedroom. That was as good a place as any to look. When they got to the double doors, she handed the flashlight to Lucy and began tugging on the handle. "It's locked. Maybe the contractor accidentally locked it on the way out – or had someone else been in the house since then?

In Lucy's mind, this was a sign from above that they should leave. "Guess we better go since we can't get in..."

Gloria wasn't going to give up that easy. There had to be a way in. She glanced around. Her eyes shifted to the top of the wooden door frame before looking back down the hall. "Grab that chair and bring it over here."

Lucy reluctantly obeyed as she picked up the chair and carried it over to where Gloria was waiting. Gloria dragged the chair to the center of the double door and climbed on top of the padded seat. She grabbed hold of the door frame with one hand to steady herself as she felt the top of the frame with the other. "Bingo!"

She pulled her hand back down. In it was a long, brass key. She hopped off the chair, shoved it to the side and inserted the key in the door. The key was a perfect fit. The door creaked loudly as it swung open. "Where there's a will, there's a way!"

The girls stepped just inside the doorway as Lucy shined the light around the dark room. "Now what?"

Gloria made a beeline for the secret door leading to the bathroom. "Follow me." She lightly pressed on the wall. The door swung open effortlessly.

Lucy flashed a beam of light around the large room. "Wow. This is right out of the movies."

Gloria flipped the switch on the wall. Bright light illuminated the entire room.

Lucy shoved the flashlight in her back pocket and began yanking cabinet drawers open. She wanted to get this over with as quickly as possible.

Meanwhile, Gloria focused her search on the shower and toilet. She lifted the lid on the back of the toilet. A musty smell filled the air. She wrinkled her nose and shook her head in disappointment. There was nothing.

Lucy quickly finished her search. "This place is clean." Gloria turned off the bathroom light and slowly pulled the door shut behind them. It would take forever to search every inch of this house and they didn't have forever.

She was halfway to the bedroom door when another thought occurred to her. What if the money was under the mattress? Such an obvious place would make it a not-so-obvious place to hide a stash of cash. She grabbed the flashlight from Lucy and headed over to the bed. She yanked the covers back and lifted the mattress.

Lucy had had enough as she impatiently waited by the door. They were running on borrowed time, of that she was certain.

A dejected Gloria slowly crossed the bedroom floor as she started to make her way over to Lucy. It was then she heard a loud creak.

Gloria shined the light down at the faded blue Oriental rug beneath her feet. She took another step. *Creak.* "The floorboards are loose." She rocked back and forth on the bottom of her foot. "I saw an old detective show once where the thief hid a bag of jewels under the floor boards."

She grabbed the corner of the rug and pulled it back. One of the boards had a gap. Gloria wiggled her finger between the gaps and pulled. The loose board easily popped out.

She tossed it to the side before grabbing a second board and giving it a little yank. She set that one to the side as she worked her way across the wood floor. By the time she was done, five good-sized floor boards were sitting in a small pile on the floor.

She swallowed nervously as she handed the light to Lucy. They both leaned over and peered down into the gaping hole. A large, brown paper bag was tucked neatly in the opening. Gloria plucked the bag from its hiding place and set it on the floor beside them. "Should we open it?"

"Are you crazy? Of course we have to open it!"

Gloria slowly unfolded the top of the bag. She leaned forward as she shined the light inside. Lucy's hand flew to her mouth as she drew in a sharp breath. The bag was filled with cash.

Gloria shut the bag and jumped up. "We found the money." Her heart was thumping loudly in her chest. She glanced around frantically. "We need to get out of here."

Lucy scrambled to her feet and practically ran to the bedroom door.

"Wait! We have to put the boards back where we found them in case the killer comes back." Gloria whispered in a loud voice.

Lucy stopped in her tracks. She turned and retraced her steps. The girls carefully set each board back in its original spot and rolled the rug over the top.

They moved soundlessly through the bedroom, slowly closing the bedroom door behind them and locking it. Gloria replaced the key on top of the trim and then carried the hallway chair back to its original spot.

The girls retraced their steps through the house and back out the kitchen door. Gloria shoved the flashlight in her pocket and headed down the steps. With only a trace of moonlight to light their way back to the alley, the trip seemed to take forever. In the distance they could make out the faint outline of the shrubs.

Out of nowhere, a small yapping dog jumped through the bushes. His barks ripped through the quiet night like a cannon going off.

Lucy put a finger to her lips, trying to quiet the mangy mutt. "Shhhhhh!!!!"

Gloria crept to the overgrown hedge. She flung the thorny bushes aside and forced her way through the narrow opening as the yapping intruder nipped at her heels.

"Come on!" She held the prickly bush open while Lucy squeezed through, snapping them shut just before the half-crazed dog attempted to follow them. His barks echoed down the alley as they made a run for the car.

Gloria tossed the paper bag at Lucy as she gunned the engine and threw it into drive. Gravel flew from the tires as Gloria peeled out of the alley and onto the main road.

Lucy snapped her seatbelt in place as she nervously glanced in the side mirror, certain at any moment police lights would be roaring up behind them. "Now what?"

That was a good question. Gloria shook her head. "Let's go back to my house." She made a quick left and stomped on the gas as they raced back to the house.

Gloria careened into the drive. The car came to an abrupt halt beside the house. In one quick move, she had her seatbelt unhooked and grabbed the door handle. "Ready?"

Lucy took a deep breath and nodded. "Yeah." As if someone were hot on their heels, the girls sprang from the car and bolted up the steps two at a time. Once inside, Gloria locked the door and leaned against it.

She glanced at the clock. It was 9:30. She grabbed the cell phone from her purse and dialed Paul Kennedy's number.

"Good evening, Gloria." Gloria's heart was pounding like a set of Tom Toms during an Indian war dance. She wasn't sure if it was from sound of his voice or the fact that she had in her possession a pile of cash that someone wanted desperately enough to kill for.

"Okay, considering." She skipped the pleasantries and got right to the point. "We have the money that Arthur Blackstone stole from the bank."

Paul shook his head in astonishment. Somehow, that didn't surprise him. "Where are you?"

"At my house with my friend Lucy. She helped me find it," Gloria explained.

Kennedy grabbed his jacket and headed for the station door. "I'm on my way. Keep the doors locked!"

That wouldn't be a problem. There was no way she was letting anyone in unless it was a handsome, gray-haired officer that just so happened to make her pulse race.

Lucy pulled out a kitchen chair as she nervously patted Mally's head. "At least we have a guard dog."

"Yeah, she'll lick them to death!" Gloria peered out the window and then yanked the shade down. She flipped the brown paper bag over and dumped the contents out on the kitchen table.

There were stacks of banded cash. She plucked one from the pile and turned it over in her hand. "These are hundred dollar bills."

Lucy picked up another pile of green from the table. "This one, too."

They rummaged through the mound. "These are all hundred dollar bills."

"I wonder how much money is here..." Gloria booted up her computer and started typing. "There are more than ten in a bundle?"

Lucy fanned the bundle in her hand. "Yeah, a lot more."

After a couple quick clicks on the keyboard, she turned back to Lucy. "From what I can tell, there are 100 bills in each stack. That means each one is ten grand."

Lucy quickly counted the piles. Her eyes grew wide. "That's $450,000!!"

Lucy clutched her chest. She let out a shriek at the light tap on the door.

Gloria peeked out around the corner of the blind before swinging the kitchen door wide open. A tall, attractive officer with salt and pepper colored hair stepped inside.

Lucy's studied the stranger out of the corner of her eye. Her sharp gaze didn't miss a thing. *So this was Gloria's new beau. My, my. She sure knows how to pick them.*

Gloria nervously wiped her brow. "Thanks for coming here on such short notice." She turned to Lucy. "Paul, this is my best friend and partner-in-crime, Lucy."

A dimpled smile greeted her as he offered his hand. "So you're the infamous Lucy. The one that manages to get dragged into Gloria's sleuthing," he added.

Lucy jumped out of the chair. "Yep, that would be me." She wasn't sure if he meant that as a compliment or not. Judging by the smile on his face, she would take that as a positive.

He pointed at the necklace hanging around Gloria's neck. "Is that what I think it is?"

Gloria completely forgot about the necklace. She reached up and started fiddling absentmindedly with the gadget. "Lucy thought the medical alert necklaces might come in handy if we got in a pinch."

So distracted by the sight of Paul Kennedy, Gloria accidentally pushed the alert button.

"Dispatch. What is your emergency?"

Lucy stomped over and snatched the necklace from Gloria's neck. She shouted into the mini-speaker. "Sorry! False alarm!"

Gloria's face warmed like a burner on high. "Sorry Lucy."

Kennedy's gazed wandered over to the piles of cash on the table. He reached down and picked one up. "I can't wait to hear how you found this."

Lucy poured water in the coffee pot as Gloria told him the story. He shook his head as she wrapped up. "We're not sure if anyone spotted us or not. The yapping dog was a dead giveaway."

"Not only could you have gotten arrested for trespassing, you could've been killed!" He looked around the kitchen. "What if the killer was staking out the house and watched you traipse out of that place with a large paper bag?"

Gloria hadn't spent a lot of time thinking about that. In the heat of the moment it was hard to focus on those kinds of small details.

Lucy handed Paul a piping hot cup of coffee. He took a sip before pointing at the pile of money. "I'll have to take this with me."

Gloria nodded in a surreal Déjà vu sort-of-way. A repeat of when she helped solve the Malone mystery that freed Andrea and helped track down the real killer. "Yes, of course."

He shoved the stacks of bills back into the bag and turned to go. "So we're still on for tomorrow night?"

Gloria blushed and nodded shyly. It was a look that Lucy didn't miss. Her friend was definitely gaga over this guy. Good for her. She'd been alone long enough and he seemed nice enough, especially considering he put up with Gloria's nosy detective work without getting too mad at her.

Gloria watched him pull out of the driveway before turning to Lucy, her face still beaming brightly at the sight of the officer. "I guess I better get you home."

Chapter 6

Jill made good on her threat, uh, promise to help her mom pick out an outfit for her date when she showed up unexpectedly on Gloria's doorstep the next morning. She hung her jacket on the kitchen hook as she studied her mom's neglected mop of hair critically. "Maybe we should have your hair done."

"Oh, I don't think that's necessary...." Gloria trailed off.

But Jill wouldn't take no for an answer. Three hours later, Gloria was staring back at someone she barely recognized. Not only had the salon cut, colored and styled her hair, they'd done her make-up and nails at the same time.

Jill twirled her mom around in the chair. "You look like a million bucks!"

Gloria barely recognized herself as she peered in the mirror. "More like $450,000."

"Huh?"

Gloria smiled innocently. No sense in getting Jill all worked up about the newest case.

She settled the bill and made her way out onto the street. Jill's stomach was rumbling. "How 'bout grabbing a bite to eat before heading home?"

There was a burger joint around the corner. Gloria picked at her food, barely touching any of it. *Must be the date tonight,* Jill thought to herself.

That wasn't it at all. Gloria's mind was preoccupied with the murder – and the money. She was also thinking about the Blackstone that checked out of the Green Springs Inn. "Do you mind if we make a quick stop over at Green Springs Inn?"

Now why on earth would her mom want to stop at the local motel? Jill shrugged her shoulders and nodded. She'd find out soon enough.

They pulled in an empty parking spot near the entrance. Gloria jumped out of the car and headed for the door. Curious as to what exactly her mother was up to her, Jill followed her inside.

The same desk clerk Gloria spoke with before suddenly appeared behind the counter.

Gloria set her purse down on the gleaming glass top. "I was here the other day and showed you a room card."

The woman groaned inwardly. "I remember."

Gloria stuck her elbows on the counter and leaned forward. "Is there any way to check your phone records to see if any incoming or outgoing calls were made to that room during that time?"

Jane Jackson, the desk clerk, nodded. "Yes, I'm sure I could find that out..." She glanced over at Jill. The nosy woman was with a different person this time. What was up with this lady? Was she some kind of undercover cop? "I don't think I'm allowed to share that information with you..."

Gloria unzipped her purse, plucked a $20 bill from her wallet and set it on the counter. "Now can you?" She'd seen someone do this once in a movie and it actually worked.

The woman picked up the bill and turned it over. It didn't look counterfeit. "I'm not sure. Maybe..."

Gloria took another $20 from her wallet and set it on the counter in front of the woman. "What about now?"

The woman snatched the other $20 off the counter and quickly shoved both bills in her pants pocket. She nodded at Gloria. "Yeah, I think I can take a look at the records." She eyed Jill suspiciously. "Just this once..."

It only took a couple clicks of her mouse before Jane nodded. "There was one call made from the room during that time." She grabbed a sticky note from behind the counter and scribbled some numbers down.

She glanced nervously behind her before handing the piece of paper to Gloria. "It lasted around a minute and a half," she whispered in a low voice.

Gloria studied the numbers before shoving the paper into her purse. "Thank you, uh, Jane.

You've been very helpful." Without saying another word, Gloria made her way out of the small lobby and towards the car.

Jill was right behind her. "What on earth was that all about?"

Gloria started the car before glancing over at her daughter. Judging by the expression on her daughter's face, she was a tad bit irritated. Gloria sighed. "It's too complicated to explain."

"Well, obviously it has something to do with the dead guy in the old Johnson place."

"Mmhmm."

But that was about all Jill could drag out of her mother. Gloria quickly changed the subject and began talking about her date that night.

So distracted by the slip of paper in her purse and who that number might belong to, Gloria nearly drove right past her own driveway.

"Mom, we're here!"

Gloria snapped back to reality. She jerked the wheel in a hard right and careened into the driveway.

Jill didn't bother coming inside. Instead she gave her mom a quick hug, told her to have a good time on her date and stay out of trouble. In other words, stop snooping around where she shouldn't be.

It was too late for that. Gloria was knee deep in her investigation. She just had to know who killed that poor man in the shed. Even if the victim himself was a criminal.

Gloria hung her jacket on the kitchen hook and made her way over to the computer. Puddles was sound asleep on the chair. She picked him up and settled him back on her lap as she carefully typed in the telephone number. She hit enter and held her breath. Whoever Arthur Blackstone called that day had something to do with his murder.

An address popped up on the screen within seconds. It was at that exact moment Gloria's heart sunk. A wave of nausea swept over her. Gloria couldn't believe her eyes. This had to be wrong.

There was no way this could be the right number. She glanced at the scrap of paper in her hand and then back at the screen as she checked again. But it was right. The business that popped up on the screen was Malone Insurance Agency in Green Springs, Michigan.

She abruptly set Puddles on the floor and wandered aimlessly into the kitchen. She went back to the computer and stared at the screen again. How was this possible? Why did Arthur Blackstone call Andrea Malone's insurance office just days before he died?

A swirl of questions twirled 'round in her head. Was Andrea his killer? Did she hire a hit man? Was it really a coincidence that Andrea had the keys to the Johnson house only days before Arthur Blackstone was killed and that she just happened to be the one to find the body?

Gloria pulled out a kitchen chair and dropped down with a thud. She laid her head in her hands. Her brain was spinning out of control. She just couldn't wrap her mind around the idea that sweet Andrea might be a killer after all!

She glanced up at the clock. Three hours and Paul would be here to pick her up for their date. Should she tell him what she found out? If she did, he would have to question Andrea and then she would find out it was Gloria who turned her in.

Her heart told her it wasn't Andrea but her brain had to consider all the facts that were now pointing in that direction. Maybe the gambling debt Walking Stan was talking about was one that was owed to Andrea's husband, Daniel, before his death and now she was trying to collect on it so she could buy the Johnson mansion.

The rest of the afternoon dragged by. When 6 o'clock rolled around, Gloria was fit to be tied. She wasn't sure if her nerves were shot because of the fact she was going out on a date for the first time in decades or if it was because her own dear friend might be a killer!

Paul quickly put her at ease. The quaint restaurant he picked out was in a nearby small town. The cozy inn sat on the edge of a beautiful lake. The sun had already gone down by the time they were seated by the large window facing the lake. The nearby lights shimmered off the water as it sparkled and danced, filling their view with a romantic glow.

Paul ordered a bottle of white wine to start the evening. Gloria picked up the menu. The restaurant specialty was fish and everything sounded tempting. Paul poured two glasses and handed one to Gloria. "Having trouble deciding?"

"Yeah," she admitted. "Everything sounds good."

He suggested the Mahi Mahi which Gloria was leaning towards in the first place. "That's what I'll have."

The waitress returned a few minutes later. With their orders placed, Paul turned to Gloria and raised his glass a wine. "A toast to your reward."

She took a sip and suddenly stopped. "Reward?"

He smiled. "Ten thousand dollars for returning the money."

She hadn't considered a reward but quickly recovered. "Next dinner's on me."

Paul chuckled softly. "I'll have to take you up on that."

The ride back to her farm was quiet. Paul chalked it up to her being nervous but couldn't have been farther from the truth. He walked her to the door and waited silently as she unlocked it. His face grew serious as he gazed down at Gloria. "Thank you for joining me for dinner." He softly kissed her on the lips. "Good night."

With that, he was gone. Gloria watched his retreating back as he made his way back to the car, the investigation completely forgotten in that moment.

Gloria tossed and turned all night. Visions of Andrea handing Gloria a cup of coffee laced with cyanide crowded her thoughts. When she woke the next morning, she was completely exhausted and filled with guilt. How could she possibly believe her friend was a murderer?

146

She promptly called Lucy, her unofficial crime-solving partner. After all, she had been involved every step of the way, however reluctantly it might have been.

Gloria got right to the point. "Can I come over?"

"Okie-Dokie. What's going on?"

"Everything." Gloria was miserable.

"Let me guess. It has something to do with the murder."

"I'm turning you into detective-material after all." Gloria retorted wryly.

Half an hour later, Lucy was sitting across the table from a gloomy Gloria.

Lucy crossed her arms and studied her best friend. "The date didn't go well?"

Gloria had almost forgot about the date. "No. The date was great!"

Lucy sawed a chunk of cherry Danish from the box and popped it in her mouth. "So what's with the long face and the emergency coffee meeting?"

"I went back to the Green Springs Inn yesterday to ask the clerk if any phone calls came in or went out from Blackstone's room." Gloria shook her head sorrowfully. "I almost wish I hadn't."

Lucy knew whatever was coming next had Gloria really upset. "And?"

"There was one."

"By the look on your face, I'd have to make a wild guess that it was your best friend and I know it wasn't me."

Gloria nervously fiddled with her coffee cup. "But close."

Lucy sliced another large piece of Danish. The piece was halfway to her mouth when the light bulb went on in her head. "Oh no."

Gloria nodded miserably. "Oh yes."

Lucy reached over and grabbed her friend's hand. "Who would've thought it would be your new beau." She shook her head sadly. "You hear all the time about good cops gone bad."

Gloria yanked her hand back. Lucy was never going to make it past amateur sleuth stage. "It's Andrea! Arthur Blackstone made a call to Malone Insurance Agency just days before he died."

"You're kidding." Lucy raised a horrified hand to her lips. "I don't know what to say."

And neither did Gloria.

Lucy tried wrapping her brain around this new piece of information. "Malone was running an illegal gambling ring on the side. So you think Blackstone owed Malone some money and died suddenly - before he could collect. Andrea's taken over the business now and had a hit on Blackstone?"

"That's all that keeps running through my mind." Gloria swallowed hard. "I don't want to believe it but all the evidence is pointing in that direction." She went on. "Andrea's husband runs an illegal gambling ring, he ends up dead."

"But you tracked down his real killer, his partner. Not Andrea," Lucy pointed out.

"True... Although she did find the body at the house she had access to and now I find out the dead man called her insurance office just before he died," Gloria logically pointed out.

Lucy tossed the empty pastry box in the trash. "Now what?"

"Simple. We have to trap the killer."

Lucy didn't like where this was going. "How do you plan on doing that?"

"We let it slip that we found the cash, it's in a secret location and then try to flush the real killer out."

Lucy plopped back down in the chair. "Does Paul know?"

"No and I don't want him to. Not yet."

Chapter 7

Gloria watched through the window as Andrea's sleek black Mercedes pull into the restaurant parking lot. The petite blonde hopped out of the car and nearly floated into the restaurant.

Andrea was absolutely beaming by the time she reached the booth. "I got the house." She sunk down on the hard plastic as she tossed her purse on the seat beside her.

"You did?" Gloria wasn't really surprised.

"Yep. I'm closing in three weeks. Just in time for Thanksgiving!" She grabbed a menu and scanned the inside but she wasn't really reading the words.

"What about the place you have now?" It never dawned on Gloria to ask Andrea what she lived in. For all she knew, it was an apartment.

"Daniel and I had a condo. I'm putting that on the market next week," she explained.

Gloria's friend Dot walked over to the booth. "Hello there, ladies."

Andrea smiled brightly. "I bought the house!"

"Congratulations!" Gloria scooted over so Dot could slide in next to her.

Dot stuck a fisted hand on her chin as she gazed at the glowing girl across the table. "So you're going to live in the big old place all by your little lonesome?"

Andrea shook her head. "Uh-uh. I'm going to get a dog."

She looked at Gloria hopefully. "Maybe we can find one at the same place Mally came from?"

Gloria patted her hand gently. "Of course we can, dear." It was at that very instant she knew deep in her heart there was no way this girl was a killer.

Dot jotted down their order and headed back to the kitchen. Andrea studied Dot's retreating back. "If you have a little extra time, you want to stop by the house? You know, just to take another look around?"

Gloria could see the stars in her eyes. She didn't have the heart to say no. Plus, she really didn't have a good excuse and maybe, just maybe, there would be another clue hidden inside. Anything that might lead her to the killer. "Sure, we can do that."

Andrea practically inhaled her food. Gloria wasn't sure if it was because she was in such a hurry to see the house again or if it was because she was starving to death. She was mighty thin. It looked like she hardly ever ate.

Gloria slid into the expensive leather seat of Andrea's luxury car. She'd never been in a Mercedes before. It smelled like old money and Lilacs. "What kind of air freshener do you put in here? It smells heavenly..."

Andrea popped her sunglasses on and waved a hand in the air. "It's one of those clippy things that you hide in the vents. This one's Lilac."

Gloria loved Lilac. It reminded her of her Grandmother's favorite perfume.

The drive to the house was over too soon. Maybe because the car felt like it was floating. Annabelle certainly didn't ride this smoothly. *I better get my shocks checked. My car rides like a tank compared to this.*

The sleek sedan rolled to a stop in front of the old house. Andrea perched the sunglasses on top of her head and jumped out of the car.

Gloria followed her to the gate. She glanced around as Andrea unlocked it. "I hope I'm not being too nosy but how much did you pay for this place?"

Andrea swung the gate open and motioned Gloria in. She closed the gate and headed for the front door.

Despite her firm belief that Andrea was innocent, Gloria glanced nervously back at the gate. *Why would she shut the gate while we're here?*

"Well, they wanted $350,000 but I was able to talk them down to $275,000." Gloria didn't think it was that great of a deal considering the work it needed.

"How much did the contractor say it would cost to fix up?"

Andrea stopped to unlock the front door. "For everything I want done, it'll be around $100,000. Most of the work will be on the outside of the house. There's also some mechanical stuff like updating the plumbing and electrical."

Gloria followed Andrea inside. If she dumped that much cash into this place, it should look like a million bucks when it was done.

Andrea quietly closed the door behind them. "The furniture's included. In fact, everything in here stays. The sellers don't want to come back and clean it out so if you see anything you like, let me know."

Andrea walked into the living room and began pulling the covers from the furniture. After the last piece of furniture was uncovered, the girls stood back and admired each piece. The furniture fit the room to a "T." Andrea ran a hand over the top of the vintage Victorian sofa. It looked like it had never been sat on.

After a quick glance around the lower level, the girls headed upstairs to check out the guest bedrooms before wandering over to the master suite.

Gloria held her breath as Andrea grabbed the door handle. A frown creased her forehead. "That's odd. The door is locked."

Gloria shook her head. "It wasn't locked when we were here the other day."

"And it wasn't locked when I was here with the contractor." She shrugged her shoulders. "Maybe it's just a finicky knob and it's just stuck." She wiggled the knob, with more force this time, but it didn't budge. Disappointed, she looked at Gloria. "I really wanted to look around the bedroom."

Gloria glanced up as if a thought suddenly occurred to her. "Sometimes there's a spare key hidden on top of the trim." She pointed up.

"That would be awesome!" Andrea spied the chair in the hall. She dragged it over and centered it in the doorway. She pulled herself up and teetered on the cushion as her hand felt along the top of the frame. "A key!"

Imagine that, Gloria thought wryly.

The key worked like a charm and moments later they were standing inside the spacious master bedroom. Gloria unconsciously glanced down at the rug that covered the loose floorboards.

Andrea made her way over to the massive king size bed. She carefully set the pillows on the floor beside her and folded the covers down.

If one didn't know better, you'd almost think that someone had made the bed just that morning. The large blue mattress was in almost mint condition. Gloria shuddered at the thought that one of the deceased owners may have died in that very bed. Yeah, it definitely needed to be replaced.

Then Andrea did something odd. She looked under the mattress.

Gloria couldn't help herself. "Looking for hidden treasures?"

Andrea laughed as she glanced back at Gloria. "I don't really know what I'm looking for. It certainly wasn't for another dead body."

She dropped the mattress and headed for the secret bathroom door. The room was as magnificent as she remembered. She ran a hand across the beautiful granite tops before plopping down on the edge of the tub. She glanced up at the ornate chandelier. "This is definitely a girly-girl bathroom," she sighed admiringly.

Gloria pulled out the vanity chair and gingerly sat down. No telling how sturdy something this old might be and she didn't want to break it. "So you're not at all freaked out about the body in the shed?"

"No. It is a little creepy," Andrea admitted, "but at least we didn't find him inside the house. I saw his obituary in the paper." She tapped the side of her face thoughtfully. "He kinda looked familiar. Like maybe I've seen him somewhere before."

Gloria filled her in on his identity and that the backpack was at one time filled with stolen cash. She studied Andrea's expression, searching for some kind of reaction but there was nothing. Not even a flicker. She was either one cool killer or really had no clue what was going on.

They admired the ornate bath for several long moments before Andrea reluctantly stood up. She reached over to switch off the lights. It was at that precise moment the two of them heard a muffled *THUMP*. She put a finger to her lips. "Did you hear that?" she whispered.

Gloria nodded, her eyes darting in the direction of the bedroom door. It sounded like it was coming from downstairs.

The girls tiptoed out of the room and silently closed the bathroom door before making their way across the room.

When they reached the hall, Gloria suddenly stopped. She heard the sound again. This time a little louder. *THUMP*.

Someone was definitely downstairs. They stood there nervously waiting for a third thump that never came.

Andrea grabbed Gloria's arm uncertainly. "We should probably go down there..."

Gloria nodded. She took a cautious step forward before stopping in the hall to listen again. Silence. She studied the long hall as she looked around for some sort of weapon.

A tall brass lamp was sitting on top of the hall table. She wiggled the plug out of the socket and lifted the lamp. It took both hands just to get it off the table. The thing weighed a ton! She shook her head. No way could she smash this over someone's head. She quietly set it back in place. They'd just have to take their chances.

They quietly crept down the stairs. When they reached the bottom, they paused. The front door was still closed. Just the way Andrea had left it.

Gloria eyes swung quickly from the dining room before focusing on the living room. Nothing appeared to be out of place. By the time they made it into the kitchen, Gloria had almost convinced herself their minds were playing tricks on them. That was, until Andrea walked over to the kitchen door. "It's open."

Sure enough, the door was open just a crack. It wasn't open when they walked through the room earlier. They locked the kitchen door before making their way back to the front door.

Andrea pulled the car out onto the street. "Be right back." Gloria watched as she swung the rusty gate closed and snapped the padlock firmly in place. She pulled down on the lock, as if reassuring herself it really was shut.

She hopped back in the car and turned to Gloria. "So what do you think?"

"That someone was in that house with us..." But who. Gloria peered into the yard as they slowly pulled away. She glanced in the rearview mirror. What if they were being followed?

Andrea pulled into the empty parking spot next to Gloria's car. Gloria jumped out. She poked her head in through the open door. "Make sure you aren't being followed," she warned her before shutting the door.

She watched Andrea drive off before quickly making her way over to Annabelle. She managed to get the driver's side door unlocked before Margaret pulled up beside her and rolled down her window. "Did you hear about the break-in at the Johnson place the other night?"

Gloria stuck her head in the car window. Someone had spotted her and Lucy! "No. What happened?"

Margaret went on to tell her the neighbor's dog got loose. He made it to the edge of the Johnson property when he began barking his bloody head off. When her neighbor, Mr. Slocum, chased after his dog, he spotted two shadowy figures emerge from the bushes at the edge of the alley.

Gloria shook her head pretending to be shocked. "You don't say..." Someone needed to give her an award for acting.

Margaret summed it up. "So it looks like there are two killers running around. Not just one." She glanced around before whispering. "Don't tell anyone, but police are setting up a surveillance of the house to see if they can catch them if they come back."

Well, that was good to know. Gloria sighed. Guess we won't be going back there unannounced. So much for digging around for more clues.

Back at the farm, Gloria grabbed her mail and headed inside the house. Puddles and Mally were both waiting to greet her just inside the door. It was nice to come home and have someone anxiously awaiting her arrival. The excitement was short-lived when Gloria spied the kitchen trash can that was laying on the floor nearby, its contents strewn from one end of the kitchen to the other.

She looked over at the most obvious culprit who had the decency to drop down on all fours and hang her head. She walked over to the dog, her hand on her hip. "Did you do this Mally?"

A set of guilty eyes glanced from Gloria's face to the trash can and then back again.

Gloria shook her head in disgust before grabbing the broom and sweeping up the stinky mess. "Naughty dog," she scolded her.

With Gloria preoccupied in cleaning up the mess, Mally got to her feet and slowly crept out of the kitchen, tail firmly between her legs. Gloria caught a glimpse of her backside as she slunk past the dining room on her way to her doggie bed on the living room floor. She couldn't really blame her too much. After all, she should've known better than to leave the trash out for the rascal to get into, especially if she sniffed out any food scraps.

Gloria's cell phone began vibrating. It was Paul. "Hey there!"

He skipped the pleasantries. "Why didn't you tell me about Blackstone and the Green Springs Inn?"

She sighed deeply. Lucy never was that great at keeping secrets.

"You're putting your life *and* your friend's life in danger."

"I was going to tell you," she defended lamely.

"When? After someone tried to kill you?" He had a point.

Gloria emptied the overloaded dustpan into a new trash bag. "Did Lucy say anything else?"

"Should she have?" He paused. "Gloria, is there something else I should know?"

She set the broom back in the closet, pausing for a fraction of a second before she blurted out. "Blackstone made one phone call while he was at the hotel."

"And?"

She sighed sadly. "It was to Malone Insurance Agency."

"You know what that means?"

"Yes," she whispered. It meant that he would be questioning Andrea. Again. "Do you have to tell her it came from me?" Please God. Don't let him have to tell her it was my fault. She held her breath.

"No. We can say it was an anonymous source."

She let out the breath she'd been holding. At least that was something.

Gloria hung up. Mally was impatiently waiting just outside the kitchen doorway, her tail wagging ninety miles an hour, hoping she was no longer in the doghouse. "C'mere girl." Mally trotted over to where Gloria was waiting. She was on the verge of tears as she buried her face in the dog's neck. Mally let out a low whine before she broke free from Gloria's embrace. She made her way over to the back door where she pawed at the door and let out another whine.

"Good idea." Gloria grabbed her leash and led her outside. A brisk trot around the yard helped clear Gloria's head. Nothing like fresh air and a devoted dog to cheer her up.

She spent the rest of the evening warily eyeing the phone on the wall, wondering if Andrea would call after she'd been taken to the station for questioning. When the phone finally rang, she nearly jumped out of her skin. Her sudden movement scared Puddles and Mally half to death.

She closed her eyes as she picked up the phone. "Hello?"

At first all she heard was sniffling. "Gloria, its Andrea."

Gloria's heart sank. Once again, this poor thing was in misery and it was all her fault. She knew she never should've mentioned the phone call to Paul.

"You'll never guess what..."

Oh, but she could guess. She listened as Andrea poured out the story of police showing up on her doorstep, questioning her about Arthur Blackstone's murder.

"I have no idea why that man called Daniel's office," she ended miserably.

Gloria was near tears herself. "We're going to get to the bottom of this," Gloria vowed. And she meant it.

She hung up the phone, a look of determination etched on her face. The only place she could think of that might hold any clues was the purple house down the road. It was time to stake out Walking Stan's place and Gloria had a plan. Now all she had to do was wait until morning.

Chapter 8

Bright and early the next morning Gloria climbed into the old combine tractor. She squeezed her eyes tightly shut and prayed the old girl would fire up. To her utter amazement, the engine rolled over on the first try. It had been years since she'd been inside the tractor and even longer since she'd driven it anywhere. She sent up a small prayer of thanks that she didn't have to go out onto the roads.

She eased the lumbering green machinery out of the barn. She made a hard right as she cut through the back yard, bumping along until she reached the edge of the field. At least she didn't worry too much about ruining good crops. Those were out now that winter was right around the corner.

Walking Stan's place was on the edge of the back field, directly across the street from her property. She made a beeline for the long row of trees lining the field. Gloria pulled in behind a thick cluster, turned off the motor and waited.

She grabbed her binoculars and peered at the faded purple place. Stan's van was parked in the driveway beside it. She sat there for a good hour with nary a car driving by. She was just about to pack it in when she saw the rooftop lights of a police car as it climbed over the horizon. *Oh no! I hope that's not Paul!*

In a mild state of panic, she started the old tractor and stomped on the foot throttle, willing the old girl to make fast tracks across the field and out of sight. She squeezed her eyes shut, as if somehow that might make her and the tractor invisible.

After what seemed like an eternity, she bumped back across the yard and finally pulled up in front of the barn. She quickly shut off the engine, sprinted across the driveway and darted into the house.

She yanked the door shut just in time to see a police car pull in the drive. Her heart sank when she saw Paul's tall frame emerge. It's not that she didn't want to see him. She just wished it were under different circumstances.

He tapped softly on the kitchen door. Gloria threw the door open and feigned surprise. "Well, hello there!"

"Thought I'd drop by for a minute. I was just over at Stan Blackstone's place to see if I could talk to him again." Paul shoved his hands in his pockets. "He wasn't nearly as cooperative this time."

Gloria shook her head, not the least bit surprised. "He's probably had more company in the last week than he's had in a decade."

Paul pointed in the direction of the tractor. "You drive that?"

Gloria nodded sheepishly. "Yeah. I took it for a spin." She glanced out the window. "Seems a shame to have it just sit there in the barn all these years. Maybe I should sell it."

She pulled out a chair. "Do you have time to sit down for a minute?"

"Yeah. That's about all I have. I'm still on duty for a couple more hours."

He eased into the chair and drummed his fingers absentmindedly on the kitchen table. "I talked to Andrea Malone yesterday."

"And?"

Paul shook his head. "She seemed really rattled about the Blackstone murder."

Gloria was curious on his take. "Do you think she's guilty?"

"My gut tells me no but I've been wrong before."

Gloria set a cup of coffee in front of Paul. "What about Stan Blackstone?"

"Well, at first I pretty much ruled him out." He cradled the cup of coffee. "But this time around – I'm not so sure..."

He abruptly jumped to his feet. "I have to get going. Maybe we can have lunch later this week?"

"Sounds good. Let's run down to Dot's restaurant here in town." Everyone was already gossiping about Gloria and her new beau. Might as well give them something to really talk about.

She gave him a small wave and closed the door as he drove off. She tossed around the idea of heading back out in the tractor as she fixed a light lunch. On the one hand, it could be a total waste of time, especially if Stan knew he was being watched, but on the other...

Gloria went with "the other." A few hours later, she once again climbed up in the cab of the tractor and slowly made her way back to the stakeout spot. The van was still in the driveway and the curtains were drawn tight.

This time she came prepared with a brand new detective novel she'd been itching to read and canteen of coffee in case she got drowsy. She quickly became engrossed in her book and was just getting to a good part when she saw a vehicle – the first vehicle in over an hour – pop up over the hill. It was an old Ford pick-up truck with tinted windows which seemed a little odd. Tinted windows in Michigan were almost non-existent.

The truck slowed as it approached the purple house before turning in. Gloria ducked down in the cab as she hid behind her book. She peeked over the top just in time to see the driver get out and make his way to the front door.

She grabbed her binoculars and zeroed in on the man's face. She'd never set eyes on him before. The door abruptly opened. Stan stuck his head around the corner, a grim expression on his face.

The tall, dark-haired man began waving his hands wildly as he gestured towards the truck.

Stan shook his head angrily and glanced around. Gloria crossed her fingers and prayed he wouldn't notice the tractor. She saw him look across the road and she could've sworn he was looking right at her. Or maybe it was just her vivid imagination. After all, tractors sitting in farmer's fields wasn't really that unusual.

The conversation abruptly ended. The man turned on his heel, bounded down the crumbling front steps and made his way over to the passenger side of the pickup. He yanked the door open, reached inside and lifted something out.

He was almost hidden from view on the other side of the truck. Gloria peered over the top of the metal door frame. Her sharp eye honed in on a pair of feet dangling out from underneath a dark blanket. The man struggled as he carried the limp form up the front steps. His head swung around as he looked up and down the street, right before he stepped inside. The door quickly shut behind him.

Gloria's heart was pounding. She needed to find out who that man was and who he was carrying. Against her better judgment, she crawled out of the cab, dropped to the ground and stealthily crept over to the edge of the field.

She glanced in each direction before darting across the street. She crouched down as she inched her way along the side of the old Ford truck. When she got in front of it, she ducked down and scrambled across the gravel drive towards the house. When she reached the corner of the house, she paused to catch her breath. Gloria pressed her body tight against the faded siding. *Now what?*

175

She stuck her head around the back side. The soft glow of a dim light was coming from a small window a few feet off the ground. The kitchen. She crept along the back side until she was directly under the light. She swallowed nervously as she inched upwards. At the edge of the window sill, she peered through the screened frame. No one was in sight. She stretched forward a little until she caught a glimpse of the living room. There was a brown sofa and what looked to be a pair of feet sprawled out on the end.

This wasn't going to work. The only thing she could do was try to find a small opening in the blinds that covered the back slider. Her foot slipped on a loose rock as she tiptoed along towards the faded wooden deck. She clutched the side of the house to steady herself. *This man needs some landscaping help.* The yard was nothing but a bunch of dead weeds and loose field stones.

She hoisted herself onto the warped boards and took a step forward. *Creak.* So much for being stealth. She silently peered through the one and only small crack in the blinds. The couch was in plain sight now.

"What are you doing??"

Gloria nearly jumped out of her skin as she whirled around.

Stan Blackstone was standing right behind her with a gun in his hand and it was pointed directly at her head.

"I-I...." She had no idea how to explain why she was peeping in his windows.

He reached up and roughly grabbed her arm, yanking her off the deck and towards the front of the house. "I'll show you what we do with Nosy Nellies."

Gloria swallowed hard as she stumbled along the uneven ground. Stan wasn't cutting her any slack. "Keep moving!"

They rounded the corner and quickly made their way up the front steps. He shoved her through the front door before slamming it shut and turning the deadbolt with a menacing click.

Gloria's eyes darted around the room. The man from the truck was sitting in a corner rocking chair, his eyes glittering dangerously. "I didn't know you were expecting company."

"My nosy neighbor, Gloria Rutherford."

The man rocked back and forth as he silently studied Gloria. "Another busybody," he solemnly observed. "Just like the one over there." His hand shot out as he pointed in the direction of the sofa.

Gloria fearfully followed his gaze. Whoever he carried in earlier was sprawled out on the sofa motionless.

Walking Stan marched over to the tattered blanket and yanked it off the body of Andrea Malone.

Chapter 9

Paul Kennedy tapped the top of his desk with the end of his ballpoint pen. Something was bothering him. That something was hovering on the edge of his brain.

He leaned back in his chair as he replayed the conversation with old man Blackstone. When Paul cornered him, Arthur admitted that the backpack was full of cash his brother stole while robbing a bank. That wasn't the part that was nagging at his brain. It was something else Stan Blackstone said that hit Paul's radar.

"When was the last time you saw your brother, Mr. Blackstone?"

"You mean my brother, Arthur?" He paused. "Probably been a good five years before he showed up a few weeks ago saying he was in trouble. That he robbed a bank and some people were after him to repay a gambling debt."

Paul paused, the pen poised in his hand. "Did you ever actually see the cash?"

Blackstone nodded. "Yeah. He showed it to me. Never took it out of the backpack or nothin'. I just looked inside."

"And you haven't seen him since that day?"

Stan shook his head emphatically. "Never saw Arthur again after that. Next thing I knew, they found his body in that old house in town."

It was at that precise moment, it finally clicked. Paul Kennedy grabbed his jacket off the chair and headed to the door. Time to go talk to the clerk at Green Springs Inn.

The clerk warily watched as Kennedy walked into the small lobby. "I was in here the other day asking questions about a specific guest."

The clerk nodded.

"A guest by the name of Blackstone."

She nodded again.

He leaned an elbow on the counter. "Can you take a look at your records and tell me – was the guest's name Arthur Blackstone?"

Jane Jackson popped on her reading glasses and began typing on the keyboard. She studied the screen for a second before slowly shaking her head. "No. The person who stayed here was Dean Blackstone."

"You're sure about that?"

"I'm positive. Guests have to show proof of ID at check-in. According to our records, he used a driver's license."

Paul rapped his knuckles lightly on the counter. That was it. There were three brothers. All three of them were in town at the time of Arthur's death.

The missing piece of the puzzle. Another brother. "Thank you. You've been very helpful."

He slowly closed the door and walked back to his patrol car. His gut told him the other brother – Dean Blackstone – knew something about his brother's death. There was a good chance Stan Blackstone knew something too.

He radioed the office, asking them to run a check on a Dean Blackstone. He also told them he needed some back up over at 1977 Gravel Range Road. The home of Stan Blackstone.

Stan Blackstone bent down and roughly nudged the shoulder of the motionless blonde woman. "Wake up!"

She moaned softly, her eyelids fluttering momentarily before closing again.

Blackstone wasn't quite as gentle the second time he tried. He reached down and slapped her face. "Time to wake up!"

That did the trick. Andrea bolted upright, her eyes wildly scanning the room as she tried to focus. "Where am I?"

Stan swung around to the man in the rocking chair. "You got the keys?"

The man slowly rose to his feet and pulled the keys from his pocket. He tossed them in the air. "Catch."

Stan studied the keys for a brief moment before whirling around to face Andrea.

Through the foggy haze, Andrea's eyes finally began to focus. It was that precise moment two thoughts suddenly occurred to Andrea. The first thing she realized is the man closest to her was holding a gun and second, Gloria was standing at the end of the couch with an expression of sheer terror on her face.

She started to push herself off the sofa but quickly sat back down as she grabbed her head. "My brain feels like it's going to pound right through my skull."

Stan turned to the other man. "What'd you give her?"

He smiled smugly. "A roofie."

Stan waved the gun in the girls' direction. "What are we going to do with these two?"

Gloria glanced over at Andrea. The poor thing was pale as a ghost and still holding her head. She cautiously walked over to the sofa and gently sat down as she wrapped an arm around Andrea's shoulders.

Her head snapped up as she glared at Stan. "We have no idea where the money is."

He took a step forward, hovering menacingly above the girls. "We're no fools. The money is hidden somewhere in that creepy old house."

The other man was glaring down at them now. He nodded towards Andrea. "We have her keys. Why don't we take them over to the old place? Maybe that'll jog their memories."

Stan nodded slowly. "Great idea, Dean. They better start prayin' it works." He tapped the gun lightly across the palm of his hand as he glared at Gloria. "Time to go."

Andrea slowly rose to her feet. The drug still in her system made her knees buckle. Gloria grabbed her around the waist as she tried in vain to keep her on her feet. "Here, lean on me."

A blast of cool evening air hit them in the face as they made their way out the door. Andrea gulped the fresh air. "That helps a little." She stumbled her way as far as the side of the yard before clutching her stomach and heaving violently on the gravel drive. She fell back against the side of the van. It took several long moments before she finally found the strength to crawl in. By the time Gloria climbed in after her, Andrea was flat on her back, her arm flung across her face. She was softly sobbing.

Gloria felt completely helpless as she patted her arm. "We'll get out of this one way or another." It was the "other" that Gloria was worried about.

The unmarked police van pulled into an empty cornfield a good half a mile away from Stan Blackstone's place. Half a dozen cops wearing bullet proof vests and carrying semi-automatic rifles poured out of the back. They hustled across the field without making a sound.

It didn't take long for them to stumble upon the bright mercury light beaming down on the purple wood frame structure. The small house was instantly surrounded. With extreme precision, the leader of the small group kicked the front door wide open, gun drawn. Paul was right behind him.

The place was empty. Stan Blackstone, a murder suspect, and his brother, Dean Blackstone, an escaped convict, had managed to slip away.

A thorough search of the inside revealed not a single clue as to their whereabouts. Paul walked back outside. Stan's van was gone but an old Ford truck sat parked in the driveway. Paul would bet $100 it belonged to the brother.

He ran a frazzled hand through his short hair. They could be anywhere. He slowly made his way down the front steps.

He walked to the end of the driveway and looked around. He slowly shook his head and turned to go when he took one last look back. Something across the street caught his eye. It was a tractor. He took a few steps forward and peered at the shadowy outline. It was Gloria's tractor.

He pulled the cell phone from his pocket and quickly dialed her number. It went right to voicemail. Next, he tried her house phone. Same thing.

He shouted at the men milling around the house. "We need to move! Now!"

They rushed back to the van and in no time were headed down the road in the direction of Gloria's farm. Paul hit the ground running before the van made a complete stop. He glanced in the direction of the barn before racing to the porch door. Just as he suspected. The barn door was wide open and the tractor was gone.

He didn't even bother knocking as he swung the porch door open. Somehow he already knew she wasn't there and that the house was empty.

He took a quick glance in the garage to confirm her car was there before heading back to the van.

There was only one place he could think of that they could possibly be.

Gloria prayed a simple prayer as she held onto Andrea's arm. *Dear Lord, please protect us from these evil men. The Bible says if we trust and believe in you, you will protect us from all harm.*

Psalm 91:14-15 popped into her head.

"Because he holds fast to me in love, I will deliver him; I will protect him, because he knows my name."

V.15 "When he calls to me, I will answer him; I will be with him in trouble. I will rescue him and honor him."

She squeezed Andrea's hand. "God will take care of us." She wasn't quite sure if she was trying to reassure Andrea or herself.

The van door slid open and Stan silently motioned them out. He pulled the keys from his pocket and quickly unlocked the gate. With Dean in the lead and Stan bringing up the rear, the four cautiously made their way to the front door. Moments later, the door swung open and the four stepped inside.

Stan closed the door and threw the deadbolt in place. He fumbled for the light switch. Seconds later the entrance flooded with bright light.

It was then Andrea was finally able to get a good look at them. The brothers looked even more evil and sinister than before. Andrea's stomach churned again as she swallowed hard. She faced Gloria with terror-filled eyes.

Gloria tried to give the poor thing a reassuring smile but it never quite made it. This was a scene right out of a horror movie.

Stan took a step closer, the gun glinting in his hand. "Now where's the money?"

Andrea shook her head as she stifled a sob. "I-I have no idea."

The men were quickly losing patience as Dean latched onto Andrea's arm and began shaking her violently. Gloria tried in vain to break his ironclad grip as she yanked on his arm. "Leave her alone!"

Stan grabbed the back of Gloria's neck so hard, she lost her balance and fell backwards, landing hard on the marble floor. She tried to soften the fall as she braced herself with outstretched hands. A sharp pain shot up her back. She sat there for a second in a haze of pain, her hip throbbing, before she finally managed to struggle to her feet.

"Nothing like two strong men beating up on a couple defenseless women," she muttered. Gloria didn't care if they really got ticked off. She knew they would keep them alive as long as they thought the girls knew where the money was stashed.

Stan turned around and spat on the ground at Gloria's feet. A warning that Gloria needed to shut up. At least Dean finally let go of poor Andrea's arm.

Gloria felt the cell phone in her pocket silently buzz. Someone was calling. *Please let it be Paul,* she prayed. He would be worried if she didn't answer. Maybe even worried enough to come look for her. She knew she was grasping at straws but at this point, that's all she really had...

Dean's sharp eye noticed the vibrating lump in her jeans pocket. He held out his hand. "I'll take that."

Gloria reluctantly pulled the phone from her pocket and stuck it in his outstretched hand. He promptly dropped it on the ground and stomped on it with a heavy boot.

Stan raised the gun and rested the barrel on Andrea's temple. She closed her eyes for a moment as beads of perspiration formed on her brow. She nervously wiped it away as she swallowed hard.

"I want the money and I want it now," he hissed.

"Drop the gun!" Stan whirled around. A thin, blonde woman emerged from the dark dining room. The gun in her hand was aimed right at Dean Blackstone's head.

Dean's eyes slid to the side as he caught a glimpse of the weapon pointed at the side of his temple. "You heard her, Stan. Drop the gun!"

Stan lowered his arm and let the gun fall to the ground as he stared at the woman beside Dean.

The woman's voice sounded vaguely familiar. Gloria whirled around. Her mouth dropped open when she realized who was now holding a gun.

"Chelsea Hicks..." Andrea took the words right out of Gloria's mouth. Chelsea Hicks, the woman who was having an affair with Andrea's husband, was standing in front of them.

A grin of pure evil and smug satisfaction turned the beautiful face into a mask of ugliness. "Hello, Andrea." She spat the words out of her twisted mouth.

Dean Blackstone was confused. "You two know each other?"

After the last few weeks in jail, all Chelsea could think about was getting even with Andrea Malone. It was all Andrea's fault her boyfriend, Daniel, was dead.

Chelsea couldn't believe her good fortune that the meddling Gloria Rutherford was here too. If not for her, Chelsea's husband, Barry, never would've been charged for Daniel's murder and Andrea would be the one in jail.

She couldn't have worked this out any better if she'd tried. Now she could get rid of Andrea and Gloria, make it look like the two brothers killed the girls when they got the money and then turned on each other. "So where's the money, Andrea?" Chelsea demanded.

Even though Gloria was terrified out of her mind, she had to know the truth. "I'll tell you where the money is but first you have to answer one question."

Chelsea tilted her head as if she was really thinking about it. She shrugged. "Go ahead. It's not like you'll be alive to tell anyone anyways."

Gloria glanced from Chelsea to the two brothers. "Who killed Arthur?"

Stan began answering in riddles. "She who holds the gun, holds the answer."

"Arthur owed us a lot of money," Chelsea explained. "Now that Barry's in jail, I need the cash so I can pay the money-grubbing attorneys."

She jabbed the gun in Gloria's chest. "This is all your fault!" She turned to Andrea. "And hers!"

Chelsea's face turned beet red. She blamed Andrea and Gloria for everything and now they would pay with their lives. "Now where's the money?"

Gloria had an idea. It wasn't a solid plan yet but at least it was a start.

"Why don't we try the master bedroom first?" She tried speaking as confidently as possible. "That would make the most sense. If I were going to hide money, I'd probably hide it in the master bedroom..."

Andrea nodded nervously, desperate to go along with whatever Gloria was concocting. "Me, too."

They slowly crept up the stairs as they made their way to the second level. Gloria turned left and with determined steps, set off in the direction of the master bedroom. Inside the room, Gloria flipped on the lights as she made her way over to the master bed. "Maybe Arthur hid it under the mattress?" she threw out hopefully.

With a slight nod of her head and a wave of the gun, the girls pulled back the sheets and blankets before slowly feeling around the edge of the bed. Gloria stopped when she got to the far end. She grabbed Andrea's hand underneath the mattress, tugging on it. Andrea scooched over so the two of them were standing close together.

"I feel something lumpy right about here." Gloria pointed as the girls moved away from the bed.

The brothers stepped forward and cautiously lifted the heavy mattress. Chelsea leaned forward, still clutching the gun in a death grip.

With their attention momentarily diverted, Gloria grabbed Andrea's arm and made a dash for the secret entrance to the bath. She swung the door open, dragged Andrea inside and slammed it shut. She wasted no time in throwing the heavy bolt in place.

"Get the chair!" Gloria yelled.

195

Andrea snatched the ornate metal dressing table chair from under the make-up counter and dragged it over to the door. With the door securely locked and the chair wedged tightly under the knob, Gloria raced over to the bath. There was a large picture window in front of the tub that was boarded shut. "We need to get this off."

Just then, the girls heard a woman scream followed by a dull thud.

Seconds later, the brothers began pounding on the outside of the door. Dean's muffled threat seeped through the door. "Open this door or we'll start shooting."

Gloria glanced around the room. "I remember seeing some wire hangers in one of the drawers." Seconds later, Andrea was back with a couple heavy-duty hangers.

Gloria took one of the hangers from Andrea's hand and began bending it into a hook. She wedged the metal between two pieces of board and began prying it off. The wood easily splintered, leaving a large gap.

She threw the hanger down and began ripping the board from the window with her bare hands.

Andrea was right next to her now, tearing away at the other flimsy piece of wood. God was surely on their side.

Moments later, the glass pane window was completely exposed. Andrea quickly unlatched the lock and threw the window open. Brisk evening air rushed in.

"Thank you, Jesus." Gloria felt like crying.

The door was rattling hard as the men tried kicking it in. When that stopped, several gunshots rang out on the other side. The two thugs were making good on their threat to shoot their way inside.

Gloria stuck her head out the window where another miracle materialized. There was a small, sloping roof right outside the window. Andrea gingerly stepped onto the ledge.

Gloria stuck her arm out. "Wait!"

Sitting in the corner of the tub was a bottle of body lotion and it was almost full.

Gloria grabbed the bottle and headed for the window. "OK, let's go!"

There was one minor problem with the roof. It was slanted downward at a precariously steep angle. They both clung to the wall as they carefully inched their way along the sloped metal roof.

In the distance, Gloria could hear sirens in the still of the night. They were very faint but they were there. Gloria squeezed her eyes shut and whispered a small prayer. "Hopefully, we're about to be rescued."

Gloria could hear the chair rattling angrily against the bathroom door. They were almost out of time!

She quickly unscrewed the lid on the body lotion and began pouring gobs of it on the slanted metal roof, right in front of the window. She finished dumping the last little bit on the roof at the exact moment the bathroom door finally gave way and the two men came crashing through.

The girls pressed their bodies tightly against the outside wall and held their breath.

Seconds later, Stan's head popped out the window. His gaze quickly honed in on the two terrified women. He leaned forward and desperately tried grabbing the edge of Gloria's jeans. She was just out of reach. He hoisted himself out onto the roof and took his first step. By the time he realized the surface was slicker than a greased pig, there was no turning back. His feet quickly gave way as he landed hard on the metal roof. He lost his grip on the gun which flew out of his hand and disappeared over the edge of the roofline. He tried in vain to grab onto something but everything he touched was covered in thick slime.

Although their situation was more than a little precarious, Gloria couldn't help laughing at the look on Stan's face when he realized he was going for a little ride. Right down the side of the roof and onto the ground below. "Help!" was all he got out before he disappeared out of sight.

Dean was right behind him as the other brother climbed onto the roof. He was doing a little better job of managing to stay on his feet. But only slightly better. His arms flailed wildly in the air as he struggled to stay upright. He reached back to grab hold of the window frame which was now just outside his grasp. His efforts were futile. Seconds later, he landed on his rear end and followed the same path as his brother, screaming loudly all the way down.

Andrea readjusted her grip. "Maybe we should..."

Just then, floodlight filled the yard as several dark figures emerged from the overgrown hedge. "Freeze!"

The two thugs scrambled to their feet and reluctantly raised their hands high in the air. Minutes later they were surrounded by men dressed in combat gear, waving guns.

Paul Kennedy stepped out of the shadows. Gloria nearly fainted. "Up here!" With one hand, she held the side of the house in a grip of death. With the other she began waving frantically.

He glanced around before finally noticing the girls clinging to the side of the house.

A ladder quickly materialized and was propped against the side of the house. Gloria dropped to her knees and slowly crawled across the bumpy roof top to safety. Andrea followed her lead and moments later both girls were safely on the ground.

They got there just in time to see the two brothers being cuffed and led away.

Gloria's whole body was shaking as Paul wrapped her in a hug. "How did you know we were here?"

He looked back at the men as they were loaded into the back of the cop car. "Something Stan said to me earlier today clicked in my brain. He said something about his brother but made it seem like maybe he had more than one..."

"So I went back to the hotel and asked a few more questions. That's when I found out the person staying there was Dean Blackstone – not Arthur."

"I got a search warrant for his house. By the time I got there, he was gone and there was a strange vehicle parked in the driveway. I knew something was up."

He turned back to Gloria. "Then I noticed your tractor on the edge of the field."

Gloria looked sheepishly. "Yeah, I was doing a stakeout when I saw the brother carry Andrea into the house. I tried to peek in the windows and Walking Stan caught me."

Andrea shuddered involuntarily. "If not for Gloria, I'd be dead right now."

Gloria pointed to the upstairs bedroom. "You better send your men inside. There's one more person you're going to want to talk to."

Somehow Paul wasn't surprised. He glanced towards the house. "I'll go check it out myself." He waved to a couple officers nearby. The three men headed towards the door.

Andrea watched them go. "Can you believe it? Chelsea again." She glanced at Gloria. "Do you think they killed her?"

Gloria looked at the two brothers glaring at them from the rearview window of the cop car. "No. I don't think they would've killed us either. At least I'd like to believe they wouldn't."

"So Chelsea poisoned Arthur Blackstone?"

Gloria nodded. "She must've been the one. She's one bad seed, that's for sure."

The girls watched as a cuffed Chelsea Hicks emerged through the front door. She yanked her arm from the officer's grip and stomped over to where Gloria and Andrea were watching from the edge of the drive. "This isn't over. Not by a long shot."

Seconds later, she was shoved into the back of a second police car. Chelsea glared at them from the window until she was out of sight.

Andrea shivered. "I'm not sure I'll ever feel safe with that woman still alive."

Caught up in the conversation, Gloria failed to notice all the reporters that were milling about. The last thing she wanted to do was talk to a camera crew.

She took a step back as she tried her best to slink into the shadows but it was too late. The news crew got a good shot of her face before shoving a microphone in front of her.

"This is Alex Jenkins from WMG News. I'm here in the small town of Belhaven where three suspects have just been arrested in the murder of Arthur Blackstone."

"With me now is Gloria Rutherford." He turned to Gloria. "Is it true that for the second time in as many months, you've solved a local murder?"

Gloria stood there staring blankly at the camera. She wasn't prepared for this. What did her hair look like?

It was obvious the woman wasn't going to say a single word. The reporter sighed and turned to Andrea. Andrea had the good sense to pat her hair down and straighten her clothes while the camera was on Gloria. "Is it true that you found not only the murder victim right here on this property but also helped solve the murder case?"

"Why I-uh..." And then she froze. The camera and bright lights were too much.

The reporter slowly moved to the side until the camera was zoomed in on just him. "Folks, if you're just tuning in, three suspects have been arrested in the Johnson Mansion murder case. We hope to have a full story for you on tomorrow's early show."

He turned off the microphone and walked back over to where the girls were still standing. "I'd sure like an exclusive interview with you. This story is fascinating."

Gloria glanced at Andrea uncertainly. Did they really want to put themselves through this?

He looked at them pleadingly. "This is my first assignment. A story like this could jump start my whole career."

Gloria sighed. She always was a sucker for the underdog. "It's OK with me if it's OK with Andrea."

Andrea nodded faintly. "But first I want to make sure I don't look like a total wreck."

The girls headed back in the house and up the stairs to the master bath. Gloria was almost afraid to see what kind of mess the Blackstones left behind when they broke down the bathroom door.

The damage wasn't too terribly bad. The door was beyond repair but that was pretty much the extent of it.

Gloria walked over to the mirror. She didn't look nearly as frazzled as she'd envisioned. Maybe she was getting used to catching criminals.

Half an hour later, the interview was over. They rode silently back to Gloria's house in the back seat of Paul's police car.

He glanced in the rearview mirror. "I hope you two learned your lesson."

Fat chance, Gloria thought. She was getting pretty good at this detective thing. "What I was really thinking is maybe the police department should hire me."

He sighed heavily. Not the answer he'd hope to hear. But it wasn't all bad. That just meant he'd be able to keep an eye on her himself.

Paul dropped Gloria off first. He rolled the window down as she made her way up the steps. "I'll call you later, after I drop Andrea off."

Gloria yawned loudly as she nodded her head. All the excitement finally took its toll.

Mally was anxiously awaiting her return. She wasn't sure if the dog was happy to see her or if it was more that she had to make a fast trip outdoors. Gloria was too exhausted to hook her to the leash. She opened the door and shook her finger in warning. "No funny stuff! Do your business and get back here – Pronto!" She could've sworn the dog nodded before scrambling down the steps.

Gloria peered into the darkness as she tried to follow Mally's movements but it was no use. She could hear her rustling around but she moved so fast it was like trying to follow a speeding bullet.

"C'mon. Time to come back in."

"Woof!" Seconds later, Mally bounded back up the steps, an ear of corn firmly clenched in her mouth.

She stuck her hand on her hip. She was too exhausted to put up a fight tonight. "Ok, you can bring it with you. But just this one time," she warned.

She quickly locked up the house and dressed for bed. She was just about to crawl in when the phone rang. "Did Andrea make it home safely?"

Paul's deep voice echoed through the phone. "Yes. I think she's relieved the whole thing is over." He sighed. "I wish you felt the same way...."

But Gloria didn't. The more cases she solved, the more she loved it. It was becoming an addiction.

"You'll need to come by the station in the morning to give a statement."

"I'll see you then?" she asked hopefully.

Paul laughed. "Of course. I have to keep an eye on you!"

Gloria hung up and crawled into her warm, comfy bed. Seconds later, Puddles crept over and curled around Gloria's head. Not to be left out in the cold, Mally jumped on board, sprawling out on the other side of Gloria and taking up at least half the bed.

She smiled contentedly as she drifted off to sleep.

Chapter 10

Gloria's foggy brain vaguely registered her phone ringing. Insistently. She covered her head in an attempt to muffle the sound but it wouldn't go away. Eventually, it stopped. She uncovered her head and glanced at the clock. Ten-ten. She lay there for several long moments as her brain worked hard to process everything that transpired the night before.

Until the phone began ringing again. She shooed Puddles out of the way. She slipped on her slippers and made her way to the phone, half hoping it would stop before she got there.

"Hello?"

"The press won't leave me alone!" It was Andrea on the other end and she was more than a little aggravated. "They're camped outside my house!"

"Hang on." Gloria set the phone down and made her way over to the window. She peeked around the edge of the long, billowy curtain that faced the street. Nothing.

She shuffled out to the kitchen and peered through corner of the blind. A news van was parked in her drive. A camera crew and reporter were lounging around out in the driveway.

She sighed. "Mine, too."

"Ugh! I can't even leave my house!"

Gloria filled the coffee pot and turned it on. "Want me to come get you?"

Andrea giggled. "So the camera crew can follow you to my house and we'll have even more of them parked outside?"

Yeah, Gloria had to admit that probably wouldn't be a good idea. "You could call the cops, tell them the reporters are trespassing."

"I thought about that but what if they write something bad about me?" She paused. "Hey, it looks like they're leaving."

With a promise to check in later, Gloria hung up the phone. Maybe the guys in front of her house would give up eventually, too.

She peeked out the window before heading to the shower. The news van was still there. She sighed in aggravation. *I guess I'll just have to wait them out.*

She threw on some clothes and snuck out the bedroom window with Mally. Desperate times call for desperate measures. The dog wanted more than anything to run around the front of the house and check out the camera crew.

Back inside the house, Gloria's phone was ringing again. It was Ruth. "Do you know you have a news van in your driveway?"

Heavy sigh. "Still there, huh?"

"Now what did you do?" Ruth already had a good idea though. "It has something to do with the Blackstone murder?"

"Yeah..."

Ruth was irritated. "How come I'm never included in all the fun stuff?"

"I never knew you wanted to. Now that I know, I'll be sure to include you in my next investigation," Gloria retorted. Just a hint of sarcasm in her voice.

"Look, I gotta go. Someone just walked in." Apparently Ruth was at work.

The rest of the morning was uneventful if you didn't count the news crew camped out in the yard. Her phone rang nonstop as at least a dozen well-intentioned friends called to let her know there was a TV truck parked in her drive. As if she could miss it.

She was almost ready to send an SOS out to Paul for help in getting rid of the pesky reporters when she heard a light tap on her porch door. She peeked through the blind. It was Jill and the boys.

She quickly whipped the door open and yanked them inside, slamming the door shut as soon as they were in.

Jill tossed her mom's mail on the table. "I picked this up on my way in." She turned to glance out the window. "What on earth is going on out there?"

Gloria pulled out a chair and plopped down. "It's a long story..."

"If I didn't know better, I'd say you were having a mid-life crisis, Mom." Jill ran her hands through her long locks.

Ryan tugged on Gloria's sleeve. "Can we take Mally outside?" Mally hated being cooped up in the house all day. She was driving Gloria crazy, darting from one window to the next, barking every time she spotted one of the pesky reporters moving about. Maybe the boys could help get rid of the reporters...

She gave them her blessing and opened the door with a warning. "Stay in the yard." She glanced at the reporter headed her way. "Why don't you see if you can entertain those nice men for a while?"

"Sure!" The boys darted out the door and down the steps. Gloria left the door open a crack, curious to see what would happen.

It didn't take long before the poor reporter had Mally's leash wrapped around his legs and Tyler was reaching for his microphone. "How does this thing work?" He grabbed it out of the man's hand. Tyler puffed up his chest and faced the camera. "Are we live?"

Jill peeked over the top of her Mom's head. "That wasn't very nice..."

She stood silently as she watched her boys in action. "I give them five minutes before they pack up and head out."

It ended up being more like four tops. Right after Ryan managed to crawl into the van where he must've found a panel of buttons because the antenna on top of the van was bobbing up and down at a rapid rate. Something akin to a possessed pogo stick.

The reporter tried frantically to snatch his microphone from Tyler's hands but instead fell face first onto the gravel when Mally decided to trip him up.

Gloria watched as Ryan was carried from the back of the van, kicking and screaming. "I promise I won't touch anything else!"

The reporter was back on his feet as he lunged for the microphone. Tyler easily skipped away, just out of reach.

Seconds later, he tossed the microphone in the air and yelled to his younger brother, "Catch!"

Ryan caught the microphone mid-air, tucked it under his arm and rolled like a football player. "Touchdown!"

The news crew tackled Ryan on the ground and wrestled the expensive piece of equipment from his grubby hands. The men rushed to the van, as if being chased by the devil himself.

The boys stood there watching as the van peel out of the drive, a look of utter disappointment blanketing their faces.

They walked back to the house, shoulders drooping.

Gloria patted them gently as they shuffled back inside. "Don't worry. If we're lucky they won't be back," she chuckled.

"How 'bout some milk and cookies to cheer you up?" The news crew was quickly forgotten as the boys devoured the snack and headed back outdoors.

Jill shook her head in amazement. "That was brilliant. For once, just once, their naughtiness paid off."

Gloria was only half-listening as she sifted through the mail. There were several bright, colorful brochures from Dreamwood Retirement Village on top of the stack. "I keep getting these stupid brochures from Dreamwood, inviting me to visit their beautiful, sprawling complex." She shook her head as she glanced over at her daughter.

Gloria tapped the edge of the three-fold pamphlet on the corner of the table. "You wouldn't

217

happen to have any idea why I'm all of the sudden getting these sent to me?"

The expression on her daughter's face was one of obvious guilt. "I was hoping if maybe you took a look at the place you just might change your mind."

"You're wasting your time and they're wasting their money. I'm not moving," she stated matter-of-factly.

She grabbed the rest of the pile and quickly finished rifling through. There was an official-looking envelope from a local bank. She turned it over and pried the back open with her nail. There was a letter inside. She opened the letter as a check fell out and silently fluttered to the ground.

Jill reached down and picked it up. "What this?" She glanced at her mom in disbelief. "This check is for $10,000!"

The enclosed letter read:

"Dear Ms. Rutherford,

Green Springs Community Bank would like to present this check to you as a token of our appreciation for the recovery of money that was stolen from our bank during a recent robbery.

Your honesty and integrity are attributes rarely seen today and we will forever be grateful for them both.

Please accept this gift of $10,000 with our sincere gratitude.

Sincerely,

Steven W. Allison, President

Green Springs Community Bank"

Gloria handed the letter to Jill without saying a word. Her hand flew to her mouth as she quickly read the letter out loud. "You found the money?"

"Mmhmm."

Jill picked up the check. "That's a nice chunk of change."

Gloria shrugged. "I've been thinking about what to do with it ever since I found out there was a reward. I think I know how I'd like to spend it..."

"A newer car?" Jill asked hopefully. Annabelle was dependable and everything but she was getting old.

Gloria shook her head firmly. "No. Annabelle stays." She glanced out the window, watching her grandsons chase the dog around the yard. They were having a grand old time.

"Half of this money belongs to Lucy. I haven't talked to her yet but I'm thinking that maybe we're going to check something off her bucket list."

Jill's eyebrows raised.

Gloria glanced down at the check in her hand and smiled. "A nice long Caribbean cruise!"

The End.

Gloria's Blissful Baked Macaroni 'n Cheese

3/4 box elbow macaroni (A whole box tends to be a little too much & the dish won't be as "cheesy.")
1 large or two medium packages of EXTRA Sharp Cheddar Cheese (2-8 ounce packages or 1-16 ounce package. Cut into small cubes.
Salt
Pepper
6 Tbsp. butter
1-1/2 Cups milk (Can use any kind -2% or whole milk, whatever you prefer)
1/8 Cup All Purpose Flour

Boil large pot of salted water. Add macaroni to boiling water. Cook until done.
Preheat oven to 350 degrees.

Drain macaroni
Toss macaroni in 2 tablespoons of butter, salt and pepper to taste.
Pour macaroni in glass baking dish.

In medium saucepan, mix a cup of milk, 4 tablespoons of butter & sharp cheddar cheese.

Stir over medium heat until cheese is melted. Add a small handful of flour. Stir.
Pour cheese mixture over macaroni.
Salt and pepper to taste.
Stir until mixed well.

Add another small handful of flour. Stir.
Add milk to cover 2/3 of mixture (if you put too
much milk in, it will boil over and make a huge
mess.)

Cover and bake for 1 hour.
Remove cover and bake uncovered for ½ hour. If
top isn't caramelized, turn on broiler. Broil for 2-5
minutes or until crispy.

About The Author

Hope Callaghan is an author who loves to write Christian books, especially Christian Mystery and Cozy Mystery books. Born and raised in a small town in West Michigan, she now lives in Florida with her husband.

She is the proud mother of one daughter and a stepdaughter and stepson. When she's not doing the thing she loves best - writing books - she enjoys cooking, traveling and reading books.

Hope loves to connect with her readers!

Visit hopecallaghan.com for information on special offers and soon-to-be-released books!

Email: hope@hopecallaghan.com

Facebook page:
http://www.facebook.com/hopecallaghanauthor

Other Books by Author, Hope Callaghan:

DECEPTION CHRISTIAN MYSTERY SERIES:

Waves of Deception: Samantha Rite Series Book1

Winds of Deception: Samantha Rite Series Book 2

Tides of Deception: Samantha Rite Series Book 3

GARDEN GIRLS CHRISTIAN COZY MYSTERIES SERIES:

Made in the USA
Middletown, DE
02 September 2024

60226547R00126